KEITH PRATT

Korean Music

東 國 之 樂

Its History and Its Performance

Faber Music
in Association with Jung Eum Sa

First published in 1987
by Faber Music Ltd
3 Queen Square, London WC1N 3AU
in association with
Jung Eum Sa Publishing Corporation,
P.O. Box Central 7,
Seoul, Republic of Korea

British Library Cataloguing in Publication Data

Pratt, K.L.
  Korean music : its history and its performance.
  1. Music —— Korea —— History and criticism
  I. Title
  781.7519   ML342

  ISBN 0-571-10081-3

This book is published with the financial assistance of the
International Fund for the Promotion of Culture,
UNESCO in Paris.

Printed in Korea

This book is dedicated to Emeritus Professor Lee Hye-Ku, Doctor of Music *honoris causa* of the University of Durham, in gratitude for his inspiration and guidance.

Contents

List of Figures

Maps, Table

MAPS

TABLE

Musical Examples

Musical Recordings

Abbreviations

(Where bibliographical details are not given see Bibliographies A,B)

AAM	*Articles on Asian music,* Bibliography B
AM	*Asian music,* Society for Asian Music, New York
BS	Li Yanshou (7th century A.D.), *Bei shu,* Zhonghua shuju, Beijing 1974
DKYL	*Dongbei kaogu yu lishi,* l, Beijing 1982 pp.154-173, 'Jian Changchuan ihao bitumu'
EKTM	Lee H.K.(7), *Essays on Korean traditional music,* Bibliography A
HUCC	*Han'guk ŭmakhak charyo ch'ongso,* Kungnip Kugagwŏn, Seoul, vols. 1-, 1979-
KC	*Korean culture,* Korean Cultural Service, Los Angeles
KJ	*Korea journal,* Korean National Commission for UNESCO, Seoul
KRS	Chŏng In-ji, *Koryŏsa* (first published 1454), Yonsei University edition, Seoul 1972
MA	*Musica asiatica,* Oxford University Press, vols.1-3, 1977-1981, Cambridge University Press, vol.4, 1984
MT	Widdess D.R. & Wolpert R.F., *Music and tradition,* Bibliography A
SGSG	Kim Pu-sik (12th century), *Samguk sagi,* Kyŏngin Munhwasa edition, Seoul 1977
SKAFA	National Academy of Arts (1), *Survey of Korean arts: folk arts,* Bibliography A
SKATM	National Academy of Arts (2), *Survey of Korean arts: traditional music,* Bibliography A
SRKM	Song B.S.(2), *Source readings in Korean music,* Bibliography A
SS	Wei Zheng (6th-7th century) *Sui shu,* Zhonghua shuju, Beijing 1973
TKBRAS	*Transactions of the Korean Branch, Royal Asiatic Society,* Seoul
TPAK	Korea National Commission for UNESCO, *Traditional performing arts of Korea,* Bibliography A

Preface

The Koreans claim to be a musical people. The clearest evidence in support of their claim over the past decade has been the success of Korean soloists on the western concert circuit, whilst in Korea itself western classical and light music enjoys great popularity and western music departments in Korean colleges of music are thriving. To the outsider, such a degree of cultural progress may seem impressive and welcome, but the truth of the matter is that despite radio and television the sophistication implied by appreciation of imported habits and values is still predominantly an urban characteristic, not unlike the adoption of Chinese culture by the literati in traditional times. A better idea of the strength of musical feeling among ordinary people throughout the countryside is obtained from their spontaneous outbursts of singing and dancing wherever small groups gather together, especially on buses and at parties. This living folk music, still popular among townspeople as well as their rural neighbours, has its instrumental manifestation in the long, strident and exciting performances of farmers' music which accompany festivals of various kinds, the sort of music that is still used by the shaman to invoke the spirits as well as, increasingly, by the local authorities to invoke tourists and television cameras.

When I first visited Korea in 1972 there were few opportunities to hear public performances of the refined 'art' music of Korea and few Koreans professed a knowledge of or interest in it. Pioneering research into its history and performance had been in progress since the 1950s, largely inspired by Professor Lee Hye-Ku, Professor Chang Sa-hun, the Korean Musicological Society and the National Classical Music Institute (Kungnip Kugagwŏn), where I studied. The list of academic publications was growing, but amateur performers and the listening public had as yet few chances of benefitting from the fruits of these labours. Six years later, by the opening of the magnificent Sejong Cultural Center in 1978, public initiation into the pleasures of *sanjo, kagok, p'ansori* and full orchestral pieces of Chosŏn dynasty music was well under way, and during my most recent visit in the autumn of 1983 I saw numerous signs of the popular enjoyment of this sort of music. Today it attracts more students, more performances, larger audiences and greater applause than it has ever done.

On a lesser scale westerners have also taken increasing pleasure over recent years in the discovery of traditional Korean music. It was played at the Durham Oriental

Music Festival in 1976, probably for the first time in Britain. The first complete *kayagǔm sanjo* to be heard in this country was given at the same Festival in 1979. In 1983 a concert of traditional music was broadcast live from Seoul by the European Broadcasting Union, and in 1984 Korean music and dance received their first performance at the B.B.C. Henry Wood Promenade Concerts. On both sides of the Atlantic concerts and broadcasts are growing in frequency. By contrast, the academic study of Korean music, its history as well as its theory, has developed but slowly over the last decade. Condit (3) was the first book on Korean music ever to have been published in the United Kingdom. In partial mitigation it must be admitted that the Koreans themselves have only scratched the surface of these subjects. Most of their publications are in Korean, and few western musicologists can read either them or the Sino-Korean source material on which they draw. For my part, I do not have the technical understanding of a trained musicologist. My approach to the study of music is a historical one, stimulated by emotional enjoyment fostered by regular visits to Korea and by close involvement with musicians and their art. The visual experience has been important to me, as it has to most westerners who have come to enjoy Korean music and dance either *in situ* or in the western hemisphere. Visual images are also important to the historian, both as a source of information and as an encouragement and guide to his imagination. I have tried, therefore, both to describe and illustrate the excitement of traditional music as it lives in Korea today, and to sketch in some points of interest in its historical background. The principal purpose of this book, however, is to present an artistic impression of Korean music and some visual evidence on which historians may base further research. Some of the plates have already been published more than once. They deserve to have been, for they are first class works of art with immediate appeal to koreanists and non-koreanists, musicologists and non-musicologists alike. But in proudly reproducing the very best, Korean publishers have tended to overlook much else that is of interest and importance. My initial impression from a survey of published sources was that the illustration of music in Korean art was very limited, and that it would be feasible to compile a comprehensive catalogue of all known examples of it. Research in Korea quickly revealed the naiveté of this view and the necessity of publishing a wider range of examples. Nevertheless, the quantity of related evidence from central Asia, China and Japan does confirm the belief that music figures less prominently in Korean art than it does elsewhere in east Asia, and that Korean artists depicted it with less originality and variety than their colleagues on the continental mainland did.

My research in Korea, carried out in the autumn of 1983, took me to national, municipal, university and private museums and to a large number of Buddhist temples. These and sites of other kinds (for example, the west face of the 15th century pagoda in Pagoda Park, Seoul) yielded a list of over three hundred instances of musical illustration in stone, bronze, painting, wood-carving and pottery. A small number of further items were subsequently located in European and American collections, some of which are published here.* No systematic attempt has been made to search all the museums and temple sites of Japan for Korean works of art, although it is certain that such a task would be rewarding. Investigation of further temples in Korea would also reveal more heavenly musicians, and a number of paintings in private collections are known to depict musical performances. I do not believe, however, that the discovery of further illustrations from sources of this kind would add significantly to the type or range of those reproduced in this book. Archaeologists alone may find new materials to alter our understanding of Korea's early musical history.

I am most happy to acknowledge the generosity of the International Fund for the Promotion of Culture and the Korean National Commission for UNESCO in financing Mr. Ahn Chang-hyon's superb photographic work and I also acknowledge with profound thanks Mr. Huh Kwon's hard work on the production of the book. Unfortunately production costs have limited the number of plates that could be included and have restricted the length of the text and number of footnotes. The selection of plates has not been easy and some subjects which would have been of interest to musicologists have had to be omitted. For this I can only apologise. The principles which have guided the choice of items have been, first, that only those with clear musical detail should be included, and second, that all types of musical illustration (paintings, carvings, mouldings etc.) should be adequately represented in proportion to the frequency with which they occur. In general, only those modern works of art which have particular importance have been selected, although the re-awakened pride in Korea's traditional music has made it a popular subject for the adornment of new buildings, commemoration plaques etc.

In part (2) of the Introduction I have followed the traditional Korean custom of considering *aak,* 'elegant [Confucian ritual] music' first, *tangak,* 'Chinese music' second and *hyangak,* 'native music' third. This sequence would not be appropriate for the arrangement of the plates. Pictures of *aak* are too sparse and those of *hyangak* would dominate the collection, giving an impression of imbalance. In some cases, furthermore, it is impossible to tell whether the musicians are playing *tangak* or *hyangak.* Therefore, after setting aside the illustration of contemporary musical performance, I have defined three new categories for the arrangement of the historical and artistic subjects, 'ceremonial and official music', 'religious music', and 'entertainment music', and have chosen to reproduce a roughly equal number of pictures of each. Of course some still belong as much to one category as to another: Any music, for example, may be said to afford a degree of entertainment. However, in the first section the formality of the occasion generally shows through, whereas in the third the overall theme is one of relaxation. The first group of plates in this section shows music

---

*Further examples of Kisan's pictures of musicians will be found in the catalogue of his paintings in the Hamburgisches Museum für Völkerkunde: Cho H.Y. & Prunner G. *(1).* Another collection, also including some musicians, is in the National Museum of National History, Smithsonian Institution, Washington D.C.

being made for personal enjoyment, followed by pictures of music played for one or more listeners.

My visits to Korea were financed by the International Cultural Society of Korea and the Korea Research Foundation, to which I am naturally grateful. The late Director of the National Museum of Korea, Dr Choi Sun-u, and his staff in Seoul, Kyŏngju, Kongju and Kwangju gave me every encouragement and much practical assistance. In particular the help of the Curator of Fine Arts in Seoul, Mr Yi Won-bok, was of crucial importance. At Seoul National University College of Music Professor Hahn Man-young (concurrently Director of the National Classical Music Institute) patiently unearthed the answers to many questions. Among the many other friends and scholars whose advice I gladly welcomed were Professors Song Bang-song, Yi Byong-won and Kim Won-yong, while at the National Classical Music Institute the Assistant Director Mr Yi Song-yol kindly facilitated photographic work. Above all, three people in Korea deserve my unstinted and warmest thanks : Professor Lee Chae-suk and her husband Lee Chang-uk helped me in so many practical ways that without them this project could have been neither begun nor completed. Their friendship and generosity, not to mention their self-sacrifice and hard work, symbolise for me the very best qualities of the Korean people. Emeritus Professor Lee Hye-Ku, doyen of Korean musicologists, has been honoured world-wide for his contributions to the study and restoration of his country's traditional music, and since the 1950s no student of Korean music has failed to benefit from his prodigious scholarship. His support for the present book - an investigation which I have known since 1974 to be dear to his own heart - has been both touching and of incalculable encouragement.

In the United Kingdom I have received help from Professor Roderick Whitfield (University of London) and Mr Don Starr (University of Durham), and from Dr Peter Manning (University of Durham) who gave valuable help in the preparation of the tape accompanying the book. To all of these my thanks are due. Sondra, Rachel and Timothy have patiently tolerated my frequent absences abroad. Above all, I am happy to admit the extent of my indebtedness to my colleague Dr Rob Provine, which he alone can tell but which he would never acknowledge. His constant patience and cheerfulness in the face of persistent demands for instant scholarly answers and considered opinions has been truly humbling. He, together with my Korean friends, shares in whatever credit this book deserves, but none of them is to blame for its shortcomings. As I have indicated, the study of Korean music is but in its infancy and no attempt to describe it fully, least of all by a non-musicologist, can yet succeed according to the standards demanded of musical scholarship in the West. I make no such attempt. Nevertheless I hope that, whatever its inadequacies, this book will at least encourage others to seek and find enjoyment in the rich musical and visual arts of Korea.

Durham, England
March 1986

Romanisation.   The romanisation system used in this book for Korean is McCune-Reischauer, except where custom or a person's preference for the spelling of his or her name dictates otherwise. For Chinese the Pinyin romanisation system is used.

SECTION ONE

Introduction

HAMGYŎNG

P'YŎNGAN

P'yŏngyang
•

HWANGHAE

KANG-
WŎN

Kaesŏng
•
Seoul
•
Suwŏn
•

KYŎNG-
GI

CH'UNG-
CH'ONG
•

Kongju
•

Chŏnju
•

Taegu
•

Kyŏngju
•

KYŎNGSANG

CHŎLLA

Pusan
•

Tsushima

Map 1. The eight provinces of modern Korea

1. Korea in Its Asian Context

The Korean peninsula forms a natural bridge between the mainland of continental east Asia and its offshore islands, of which the most important are those of Japan. Scarcely more than six hundred miles separate its northern frontiers from its southern coastline, and for most of the last two thousand years those northern frontiers have been close to, or contiguous with, the north – east corner of the Chinese empire. Inevitably, the Korean people have found themselves involved in the relations between the mainland and Japan, and their way of life and culture have been disturbed and influenced by the passage of merchants, diplomats, missionaries, and worst of all, soldiers. Despite this, or perhaps because of it, they have preserved a nationalist spirit which has succeeded in maintaining independent Korean traditions as well as absorbing some of those from outside. As a united nation from 668 to 1945 A.D., the sense of Korean separateness from her neighbours, to whom she nevertheless conceded political suzerainty for much of this time, survived and occasionally flourished more strongly. Nothing illustrates this better than her music. In many of her arts the Chinese connection is more apparent than the native tradition, but in music a better balance was kept, and though its story is partly related to that of the great transmission of music from the Near East to the Far East which is one of the major themes in the cultural history of the world, it is also one of native inventiveness and inspiration creating something special in accordance with local conditions and tastes.

The living musical traditions of east Asia were formed by the confluence of two broad rivers. One rose in the Near East, and as it flowed across central Asia picked up a powerful tributary from the Indian subcontinent as well as streams from the steppes, oases and mountainous regions further to the north. It reached China during the second half of the first millenium B.C. and there converged with the second river, the strong current of native music which had sprung into being more than a thousand years earlier. Conservative Chinese put up some resistance to the foreign sounds at a time when political, social and cultural standards were all threatened by rapid change, calling them crude and licentious, but their opposition was not very effectual and from the Han dynasty onwards the mainstream of Chinese musical life regularly welcomed fresh inspiration from inner Asia and beyond. It adopted the four- and five-stringed lutes for example, which quickly became favourite instruments for solo and ensemble performance. It accepted the bowed strings, the fiddles used by the Mongol con-

23

querors in the 13th century whose own presence in China was a good deal less welcome and much more short-lived. It quickly came to appreciate the hammered strings, the dulcimer introduced by the Europeans in the 17th century which was one of the most unlikely of the permanent immigrants to the Chinese cultural scene. Music of China also responded to changes in the philosophical outlook and literary styles preferred by the literati, and to the gradual absorption into China of regions with distinctive folk musical traditions, such as those of the south-east. It developed forms as diverse as the pensive repertoire for the *guqin* and the raucous, exuberant cacophony of the opera, each distinctly Chinese yet so different and profoundly abstruse as to seem to belong to worlds apart. So when we talk of traditional Chinese music, we refer to the cumulative inheritance of a culturally sophisticated country which has incorporated the musical experiences and preferences of many peoples, Chinese and non-Chinese, over nearly four thousand years. Obviously this music changed a great deal over the centuries, but whilst literature reveals the depths of musical appreciation in traditional China, most of the music itself has disappeared, and except for a small number of reconstructed examples can no longer be heard. Some tunes which are still played may date from the Ming dynasty or earlier, but in the past the Chinese were unsuccessful at preserving or reviving the music of former times and in the present they see little need to do so. Neither do they share the western concern over authorship and date of composition.

From China the musical river wound its way beyond the Great Wall into Korea, the north-western part of which was an outpost of the Chinese empire from 108 B.C. to 313 A.D., known as Lelang. In this remote corner of the continent disunited politically and artistically unpretentious until Chinese colonists brought it the benefits of Han civilisation, the spring of native music was already beginning to bubble up, but instead of being swamped by the force of the mainland current it was fed by it and grew into a strong and distinctive musical existence in its own right. Thus the river neared the end of its epic journey in two branches. Both flowed into the waters of the Korea Straits and finally reached the shores of Japan, where some 'bottling' of the Chinese court music traditions took place in the *gagaku* tradition, but where the greatest benefit was again experienced in the nurturing of local music. Today, apart from the physical appearance of many of the instruments, there is little to indicate the substantial heritage shared by China, Korea and Japan. Their music differs to a far greater extent than does the music of any three countries within the western musical sphere, even though they rub shoulders with one another within the so-called Chinese cultural zone.

From the Three Kingdoms period until the end of the Chosŏn dynasty, in other words through the entire royal era of nearly two thousand years, the cultural ties between China and Korea were strong and the political links, through the Chinese tributary system, more regularly effective than between China and almost any other neighbouring state. At first their effects were not felt uniformly across the whole peninsula. Whilst all three pre-Unification kingdoms – Koguryŏ, Paekche and Silla – acknow-

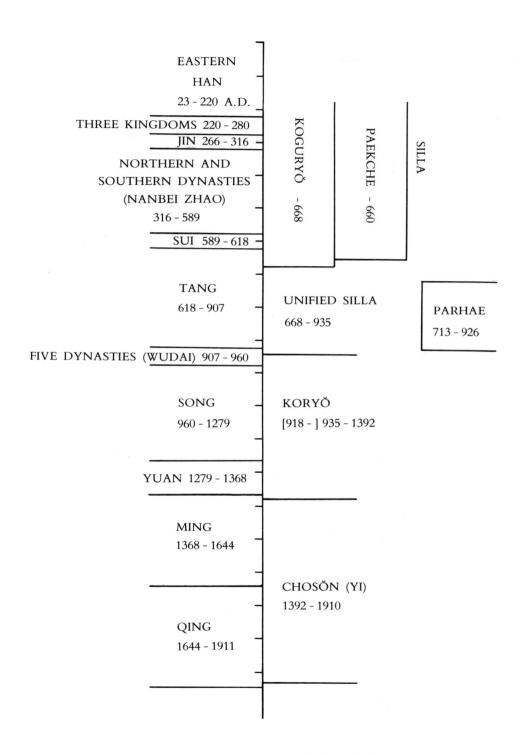

Table 1. The dynasties of China (left) and Korea

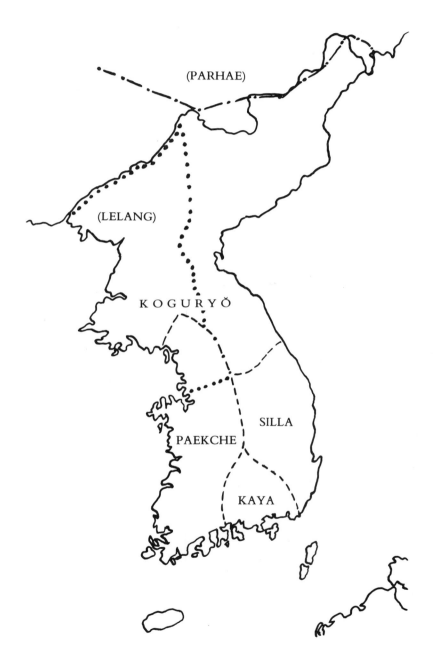

(PARHAE)

(LELANG)

KOGURYŎ

PAEKCHE

SILLA

KAYA

Map 2. The divisions of Korea before the Unified Silla period

ledged the suzerainty of China and witnessed sooner or later to the cultural influence of Confucianism and Buddhism, their arts exhibited strong regional characteristics. Those of Koguryŏ were influenced by the Chinese presence in Lelang but still reflected the fierce outlook of a border people toughened by the hard climate, the rough terrain and frequent military clashes. The people of Paekche, the south–western state, enjoyed a less tempestuous development, accepted Buddhism as their dominant experience of Chinese influence, and allowed it to imbue their art with a much gentler nature.[1] The most remote of the three kingdoms, the south–eastern state of Silla, was the least advanced artistically, though its eventual military success and imitation of Chinese political and cultural leadership show how quickly it left behind its early naiveré. Decorated end roof-tiles illustrate the different artistic levels and outlook (fig. 1). Music appears to do the same, although what we know of it at this early period is limited even in description and does not include any actual tunes.

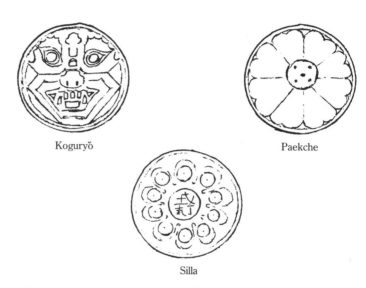

Koguryŏ

Paekche

Silla

Fig. 1 Decorated end roof-tiles of the three kingdoms

All the surviving paintings of Three Kingdoms musical scenes come from Koguryŏ, where the Chinese style of tomb construction and decoration was copied and where Chinese music was fashionable among the aristocracy. The sort of processional music (known in Chinese as *guchui,* 'banging and blowing') illustrated on the wall of no. 3 tomb at Anak fits in well with our idea of the spirited Koguryŏ nature, which is reconfirmed by its best known musical invention, the *kŏmun'go.* One of the prominent features of this instrument is the use of a short stick as a plectrum, which both plucks and strikes the strings and thus produces a sharp sound which evidently contributed a little welcome force to musical performances in Koguryŏ. Other instruments used there were adopted with little or no alteration from north China and central Asia. They were used to play north Korean music at the Chinese court following Emperor Sui Wendi's recruitment of five foreign bands to play alongside Chinese musicians early in his reign (589-605 A.D). The Koguryŏ band consisted of eighteen players. One fears for their unrecorded fate, however, when Koguryŏ armies inflicted a heavy defeat on a Sui expeditionary force in 612 and further rebuffed Emperor Yangdi's expansionist ambitions during the following two years. Their sojourn in the distant Chinese capital had probably been against their own and their families' better judgement in the first place. Chinese and Korean histories list seventeen instruments played in Koguryŏ, mentioning three drums, two oboes, two lutes, two harps and the mouthorgan, but not the long curved horn *jue*, which would not have been heard in the Sui court ensemble. The same sources reveal only seven instruments from Paekche.[2] They too came originally from China and beyond, and their inclusion of the horizontal flute *chi,* the *yu* mouthorgan, the vertical harp and the *zheng* zither, instruments which, together with the *pipa,* made up the instrumental ensemble for the *wu sheng* music of Zhejiang Province, suggests that Paekche's music arrived by way of the sea-route from the mouth of the Yangzi River (Wu & Liu (1) p.59). Judging by the range of instruments it may have been gentler in tone than Koguryŏ music. The *Sui shu* and *Bei shi* do tell us that Paekche also had 'drum and horn music' (*gu jue zhi yue*), but since the *Bei shi* specifically mentions Chinese residents in Paekche it may have been they who were chiefly responsible for its use.[3] Paekche music was not so prominently represented at the Sui court but did enjoy some short-lived recognition at the new Tang court. Once again, however, politics may have caused embarrassment to the Korean musicians when Emperors Taizong and Gaozong become embroiled in the violent relations between their three tributary kingdoms and were involved in wars against both Koguryŏ and Paekche.

During the 6th and 7th centuries Korean teachers of music, dance and masked drama crossed the sea themselves, to Japan. As late as the 9th century the Japanese history *Nihon goki* refers to the presence of four teachers of Paekche music, four of Koguryŏ music and two of Silla music, implying that regional styles of Korean music were still recognised there after nearly 150 years of political unification on the peninsula, and also apparently pointing to a lesser degree of cultural attractiveness in the heritage of the south-east. The *Sui shu* does not even accord a mention to the instruments of Silla, though it does tell us that its music was played at court in a subsidiary capacity.[4] In fairness, two substantial pieces of mitigating evidence may be offered on behalf of Silla music. The first is that in 551 A.D. a refugee from the neighbouring small state of Kaya, threatened with annexation, fled to Silla and presented its king with Kaya's own new instrument. This was the 'zither of Kaya', the *kayagŭm,* said to have been invented by King Kasil on the basis of the Chinese *zheng* zither. The refugee, whose name was U Rŭk, was evidently a leading composer in Kaya. At first the eleven pieces of his own music that he played to his Silla hosts were not appreciated and were called inelegant and improper, comments that at least imply some sense of musical standards on the part of Silla musicians. They, overcoming U Rŭk's natural objections, produced revised versions of the tunes which not only satisfied him but also earned from King Chinhung the epithet 'great music'.[5] U Rŭk's astute offering ensured the survival of what subsequently became Korea's most famous instrument. Neither of the other two states yet had it, and though its true beauty and potential may not have been immediately recognised beyond Silla, it eventually joined the *kŏmun'go* as one of the instruments of which the Korean people are most justly proud.

According to the *Samguk sagi* the three stringed instruments, *kayagǔm, kŏmun'go* and *pip'a* were used in Silla together with three flutes, one drum and the *pak* clappers. This is the second piece of evidence in Silla's defence. The flutes were native flutes, the *taegǔm, chunggǔm* and *sogǔm,* once again superb instruments which were destined to outlast the imported flutes and to become the most characteristic woodwinds in the Korean orchestra. It is hard to believe that the musicians of Silla did not respond to their potential by composing worth-while music. However, lacking the stronger Chinese element that was both recognisable and respected in the music of the two other kingdoms, it is perhaps understandable that the music of Silla should have had a hard struggle to gain acceptance over the rest of the peninsula and abroad.[6]

By the Unified Silla period the sinicized outlook of the Korean upper class demonstrated the aptness of the tag *junzi zhi guo*, 'Country of Gentlemen', which the Chinese had first given to Korea back in the Han dynasty. They used the Chinese script, read the Chinese Classics, sent students to the Imperial Academy in the Chinese capital, and established a state school of their own for the advancement of Chinese culture and political science. They observed Chinese ritual at court and organised the government into deparments along Chinese lines.[7] Even their own capital city of Kǔmsŏng, modern Kyŏngju, was laid out in chequer-board fashion in imitation of the great Chinese city of Chang'an. With an area of 80 sq. km. within its walls, an estimated population of around one million in the 7th-8th centuries, including many foreigners, and a level of upper class material sophistication now fully documented by archaeological discoveries, the imitation of the Chinese capital was by no means an inferior or an impertinent one. The court adopted Chinese dress, and even today the attractive form of high-waisted, long-skirted dress with the short, wrap-over blouse, called *hanbok* and dating back to Chinese fashion in Tang times, is still worn for best by many Korean women. It goes almost without saying that they danced Chinese dances and heard Chinese music, whether at court banquets, Buddhist rituals or military parades, and by now it was as much appreciated in the south-east as in any part of the country. By the time Buddhism had reached its peak in 8th century China it had also spread across the whole of the Silla kingdom, as may be seen today from the large number of stone pagodas, stupas, memorial stones and rock carvings dotted across the beautiful Korean countryside. Among the most favoured schools were those of Amitabha (Pure Land, *Chŏng t'o-jong),* which put emphasis on prayer *(yŏmbul),* Esoteric Buddhism *(Milgyo),* which stressed ritual, and Meditation *(Sŏn-jong,* Jap.*Zen),* which placed reliance on contemplation. In the 6th and 7th centuries there had been a particular vogue for the Future Buddha, Maitreya, among the upper classes, who had sponsored many a stone or bronze statue of him seated, pensive and one leg folded, in his Tusita heaven.

On the whole, good neighbourliness continued to prevail between China and Korea in the following centuries. Trade flourished in the Koryŏ period, and besides merchants envoys, scholars, painters and doctors travelled backwards and forwards, taking with them books, paintings, musical instruments, horses, tea, herbal medicines, and a wealth of other gifts. In 1076 a Korean embassy played music at the court in Kaifeng and two years later the Chinese ambassador An Dao presented King Munjong with ten sets of ivory clappers, ten ivory flutes and ten ivory oboes. The Korean government employed teachers of five Chinese instruments, the iron slabs (*fangxiang*), *pipa, bili* oboe, *di* flute and *paiban* clappers, and of Chinese dance and singing. It maintained a special orchestra to play Chinese music as well as the one that played Korean music. The court was scrupulous about trying to maintain its ceremonial exactly according to Chinese prescription, a policy that brought notable recognition when Emperor Huizong sent King Yejong a gift of 167 instruments and music in 1114, and 428 superb and special instruments with the music and teachers for Confucian ritual music two years later. They were probably the most splendid gifts ever made by a Chinese emperor to a vassal king, and if their political strings did not go unnoticed in Kaesŏng the Koreans did appreciate the presents themselves (Pratt (1)). Even the intrusion into the relationship of invaders from the north, the Chidan, Ruzhen and the Mongols, was in the long run surmounted. With the defeat of the Mongols and the return of a native dynasty to China in 1368, neo-Confucianism and the orthodoxy of the great Song dynasty philosopher Zhu Xi were firmly adopted in Korea as the guiding principles of the early Chosŏn dynasty. The gift of a new set of instruments from the Yongle Emperor in 1406 confirmed his appreciation of a promising situation.

At the end of the 16th century, however, came an unprecedented challenge from the east as the unifier of Japan, the great warrior Hideyoshi, sought to march across Korea in his quest for the Dragon Throne itself in Peking. His invasions in 1592 and 1596, though unsuccessful in their ultimate aim, caused immense devastation throughout Korea and put the Sino-Korean alliance under a strain from which it never really recovered its vitality. Despite an expensive Chinese gesture of military support it was the Koreans themselves who emerged with the most credit from the engagements, prompting in the bitter decades of reconstruction and reassessment that followed on the one hand a reaffirmation of conservative neo-Confucianism and on the other a hardening of independent convictions of self-sufficiency.

Any sense of relief at the Japanese defeat was soon shattered by renewed invasion, this time from the opposite direction as the Manchus swept down and conquered Korea in 1637 and China in 1644. Some Koreans reacted with a narrow, defeatist attitude, but before long the *Sirhak* 'Practical Learning' School advocated a more positive response to troubled times. Taking their cue from the 17th-18th century *Kaocheng* school of academic research in China, its members brought a new empiricism to the study of Korean and Chinese history and of the Chinese Classics. In their view, a broad conspectus of knowledge and experience would bring practical benefit to ordinary Korean people. In responding to this assertion scholars and artists, whilst continuing to imitate well-known and respected Chinese forms, also made increasing use of Korea's own alphabetic script, *han'gŭl,* and developed an attractive Korean style of *genre* painting. Musically, the court struggled to restore and maintain official music and to impress visiting envoys from Peking, but greater inspiration went into the development of two distinctive Korean vocal forms, the lyric song *kagok* and the long dramatic song *p'ansori*. Collections of court music were published in the *Taeak hubo* (1759) by Sŏ Myŏng-ung, and of popular songs in the Korean poetic tradition in the *Ch'ŏnggu yŏngŏn* (1728) by Kim Ch'ŏn-t'aek, a famous *kagok* singer. Some *Sirhak* scholars became acquainted with western musical theory, although the most famous of all *Sirhak* encyclopoedic works, *Haedong yŏksa* (late 18th century), devoted only one of its 85 books to music and this consisted entirely of accounts of Korean music from Chinese historical sources.

2. Korean Music

In the early Tang the Chinese had described music in terms of 'elegant music'(*ya-yue*), which included ritual and ceremonial court music, 'popular music' (*suyue*) and 'foreign music' (*huyue*). By this time the Koreans were well accustomed to Chinese music and gave it the title of *tangak* ('music of Tang'), in contrast to their own music and that of other countries which eventually came to be known as *hyangak* ('native music'). In 1116, long after the Chinese had ceased to bother about such compartmentalisation, the Koreans added 'elegant music'(*aak*) to their two other categories when the court received Emperor Huizong's gift of sacrificial music and instruments. Unlike the Chinese, they went on thinking of music under these three headings, and had they not done so - thereby according ritual music a specially protected status - our own appreciation of early Chinese as well as Korean ritual instruments and music might have been less vivid than it is, for the vestiges of this splendid·mediaeval culture have been better preserved in Korea than anywhere else. The music itself quickly became koreanised, and in the Red Turban rebellion of 1361 even the instruments were lost or damaged, so between 1425 and 1430 King Sejong commissioned a Deputy Magistrate in the Office of Sacrificial Rites, Pak Yŏn, to make new sets of stone chimes, tune them and the rest of the orchestra to pitches in accordance with imported Chinese chimes, and try to restore pure Chinese music for ritual use. Pak Yŏn based his revision on the music of the Yuan dynasty Chinese musicologist Lin Yu, which was believed to fit the description of sacrificial music given in the *Rites of Zhou* (*Zhou li*). In fact the results were in no way a genuine revival of ancient Chinese music but they were acceptable: Pak Yŏn's immediate reward was promotion, but his lasting memorial was the establishment of a musical form for *aak* which has survived, however incompletely, to the present day.

Some idea of the solemnity, richness, and time-consuming nature of the sacrifices of royal times can be derived from the two ceremonies which are still performed in Seoul. They are the biennial Sacrifice to the Confucian Spirits, held every spring and autumn at the shrine in the former National Academy, now Songgyun'gwan University (Provine (2)), and the Sacrifice to the Spirits of the Royal Ancestors, which takes place in the fifth lunar month in the Chongmyo shrine. Both are shorter and less complex than they used to be in the Chosŏn dynasty and their atmosphere is spoiled by the public with their cameras and tape recorders, but they are authentic survivals, not reconstructions for tourist purposes, and the attitude of the participants and the elderly members of the audience, relatives of cognate families, conveys the significance of the occasion and suggests the fervent Confucian convictions of former times. At each ceremony the music is provided by players from the National Classical Music Institute and the dances performed by boys and girls from its High School. All wear the scarlet and gold costumes, black hats and black boots of the Chosŏn dynasty court musicians. At each Shrine the orchestra is divided to play alternately, one part (called *tungga*) sitting on the terrace in front of the Shrine building itself, the other (*hŏn'ga*) some distance away on the far side of the courtyard, near the main gateway. Changes have naturally occurred more than once in both rites since 1116. In 1463, for example, King Sejo ordered the use of more *hyangak* at the Royal Ancestral Shrine on the grounds that it was more appropriate than *tangak* for the spirits of departed Korean kings. Today's orchestras are only half the size of those in the late Chosŏn dynasty and much smaller than those of the early Chosŏn when the *tungga* numbered 62 and the *hŏn'ga* 139, and it is difficult to imagine the volume produced by multiple sets of bells and chimes playing in unison, even in the open air. These are the instruments that announce the melody, and together with the percussion instruments, notably the tub, *ch'uk,* and the tiger, *ŏ,* which help to mark the opening and closing passages of musical sections, they are among the most ancient of all east Asian instruments.

Of the twelve Chinese tunes revised by Koreans for the Confucian Sacrifice in the early 15th century only two now survive, each of 32 notes. One is repeated in various keys throughout the first six sections of the ritual, the second accompanying only the seventh and final section, 'Sending off the spirits' (Musical Example 1). Each orchestra plays the tune in turn over and over again, until the conclusion of a stage of action within the Shrine simultaneously ends the music too. The music is extremely slow, solemn and regular (approximately one note every five seconds), and is played in unison, its unique feature being the way in which each note ends with an upward *glissando* on the wind instruments, producing an almost ghostly effect that is counter--balanced to some extent by the regular, down-to-earth beats from the heavy drum (Song, K.R.(1)) (Musical Recording 1).

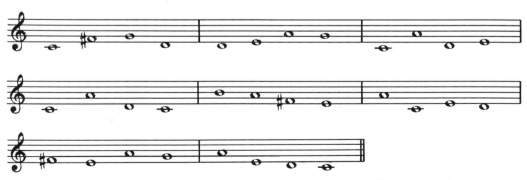

Musical Example 1. *Munmyoak,* 'Sending off the spirits'

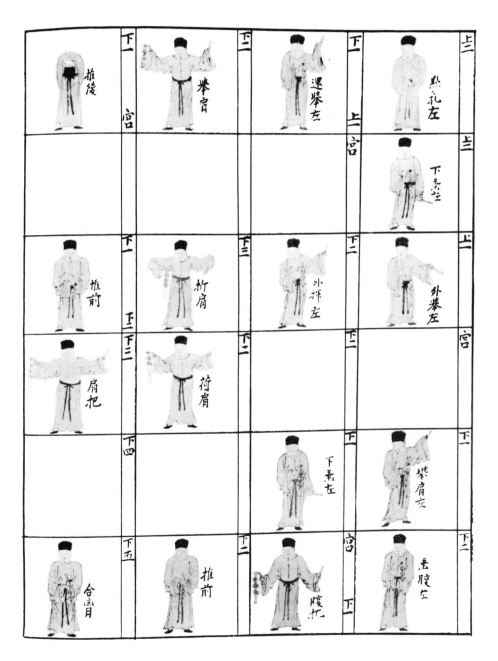

Fig. 2 Dance movements accompanying *Pot'aep'yŏng*

The music for the Royal Ancestral Shrine ceremony dates from 1463, when King Sejo selected two suites, *Pot'aep'yŏng* and *Chŏngdaeŏp*, arranged by his father Sejong from Chinese and Korean tunes for use at court banquets. Some adaptation was required to make them suitable for the accompaniment of ritual and one or two further changes have taken place subsequently, but on the whole the music played today is still that of the early 15th century. It plainly exhibits the chief characteristics of Korean ritual music, that is to say unison instrumental playing, modality, and the pentatonic scale CDEGA (except in the final section, where a tune of Chinese origin is suggested by the appearance of a heptatonic scale CDEFGAB) (Song, K.R.(2)) (Musical Recording 2). It is *hyangak,* quite unlike the *aak* of the Confucian Shrine ceremony, yet it still uses the bells and chimes of Chinese ritual music and even adds to them the iron slabs, *panghyang,* and the *tangp'iri* of *tangak.* The grandeur of this hybrid, yet uniquely Korean ceremony, is enhanced still further by the richness of the royal robes and the distinction of the pageantry.

Both rites include 'civil' and 'military' dances performed by 64 dancers, the number permitted by imperial Chinese protocol to the ruler of an empire and only authorised in Korea since 1897, when King Kojong took the title of Emperor. They stand on the left side of the courtyard between the two orchestras in eight rows of eight, and their 'dances' consist of turns through 90° and slow movements performed on the spot, using arms and legs and bending at the waist (fig.2). Two separate teams were once used for the two sets of dances but nowadays the same 64 girls simply change headgear and props to perform for the whole ceremony. In deference to modern sensitivity they are allowed to sit between sections, something that was not permitted even ten years ago when the dancers were boys, but they can nevertheless be exposed to hot sun for long periods of time. The Confucian Shrine ceremony lasts approximately two hours, the Royal Ancestors' ceremony longer. For the civil dances, performed at the Royal Ancestral Shrine to the 1st, 2nd and 4th stages of the rite, the dancers wear black hats shaped like those of Chosŏn dynasty officials; their props consist of a flute in one hand and a stick surmounted with a dragon's head in the other. For military dances, to the 5th and 6th stages, the hat is red and shaped like a fez. At the Confucian Shrine the dancers hold a wooden shield and a mallet, with which they strike it, and at the Ancestors' Shrine a wooden spear and a sword.

The sense of apartness belonging to ritual music, whether *aak* or *tangak,* is parallelled by the quite distinct and very formal style of painting which describes court ceremonies and entertainment. The necessity for formality and decorum, it seems to say, reduces people to symbols which may be lined up and moved around in different formations like metallic pieces on a magnetic screen. The musicians and dancers are nothing but characterless representations of the reality, suggesting a lack of emotion about their performance that may still be sensed in the music and ritual at the two Shrines, but which one knows to be an untrue reflection of the players' and the spectators' real sense of musical enjoyment. The artist was not expected to convey the feelings of the court any more than *aak* was intended to stir up a visible emotional reaction, though the positive effect of the music on the minds of the listeners is undoubted. The Chinese view was that music and ritual were the means of balancing the relationship between heaven and earth, of regulating the government and of cultivating human virtues, solemn matters demanding the highest possible standards and, surely, the utmost concentration by performers and observers alike. Korean scholars had studied the Confucian Classics that enshrined this belief since childhood, books like the *Record of Ritual (Li ji)* which incorporated the Han dynasty *Record of Music (Yue ji)*.

> The function of ritual and music is to bring emotions into harmony and to add distinction to conduct... When a great person promotes ritual and music, heaven and earth will be glorified as a result. At the spontaneous uniting of heaven and earth, the perfect balance of *yin* and *yang,* and the embracing warmth and enfolding protection revitalising all creation, plants and trees will flourish, seeds and buds burst forth, feathers and wings grow strong, horns and antlers spread wide, and hibernating insects awaken... So when music is played in the ancestral temple and rulers and subjects, superiors and inferiors hear it together, they will, without exception, [be united in] harmony and respect [for their leader].[8]

Koreans of neo-Confucian conviction in the Chosŏn dynasty shared these feelings. If they were seriously interested in music they read Song dynasty works which re-emphasized the same points, books like Chen Yang's *Yue shu* ('Music Book'), Ruan Yi and Hu Yuan's *Huangyou xin yue tuji* ('Illustrated Record of the New Music of the Huangyou Period'), and the anonymous *Zhou li jing tu* ('Illustrations for the Rites of the Zhou Dynasty'), all of which were widely quoted. Those who were put in charge of music at ritual and ceremonial occasions were just as aware of the gravity of their responsibilities as their colleagues in Peking were, even though the approach to government in both capitals was far more empirical and less expectant about the results of canonical magic than it had been in earlier dynasties.

When Chinese visitors were received at the Korean court they were greeted and entertained with quasi-Chinese rites and both Korean and Chinese music. Although *tangak* means 'music of Tang' it came to be used as a general term for the Chinese music of any period played at the Korean court, especially in the Koryŏ and early Chosŏn dynasties for the contemporary Chinese verse form *zi* set to music. The Korean dynastic history *Koryŏsa* lists the names of 41 *zi*, many of them love songs, of which a particular influx occurred in the 11th and 12th centuries. It is impossible to say how long the Chinese tunes survived in the alien environment. Only two pieces of *tangak* are known and played today, *Nagyangch'un* ('Spring in Luoyang') and *Pohŏja* ('Walking in the Void'), and neither of them bears any strong similarity to its Chinese original (Condit (3)) (Musical Example 2). Both are now orchestral pieces, although the words of *Nagyangch'un,* a poem by Ouyang Xiu (1000 - 1072), are still preserved:

Gauze windows glimmer and the yellow nightingale twitters.
In the fireplace some fire lingers still.
Silk curtain and tapestry hold me warm from spring's cold.
Last night it rained.

Leaning on the screen I see light-winged seeds afloat in the air.
I close my eyes, my mind disturbed.
Flowers in hand, drying tears, I ask the returning wild geese:
Have you seen my love?

Even the sound of the orchestra which may once have accompanied the singing of this song at court entertainments has changed, the bells and chimes of *aak* having taken the place of the iron slabs *(panghyang)*, and the favourite Chinese instruments the *pipa* lute and the *sheng* mouthorgan having disappeared (Musical Recording 3).

Musical Example 2. *Nagyangch'un,* 'Spring in Luoyang'
    (A) The reconstructed mediaeval Chinese tune.
    (B) The opening bars of the *taegŭm* part in the modern ensemble score

INTRODUCTION

Though there is little doubt that the upper class enjoyed Chinese songs, the preference for native music at court and throughout the country is also unquestionable, one of the features of Korean songs being the irregularity of their lines in contrast to the regularity of Chinese musical settings. By the 15th century even *Pohŏja* had become so koreanised that it was later counted as *hyangak* in the score book *Taeak hubo*. Paradoxically, the death-knell of much *tangak* may have been sounded by the neo-Confucian movement of the 15th century, which in trying to purge the court of improper elements threw out not only many of the distracting texts of Song dynasty love songs but probably the remnants of much of the Chinese music as well. Officials such as Yi Se-chwa (1445-1504), who presented the following memorial, demonstrated the strength of moral traditions learned from the *Record of Music* and similar works but also the failure of the conservatives in the Chinese culture zone to develop polemical skills beyond those of the Warring States period, when just the same kind of unconvincing objections had been loudly raised to popular music imported from central Asia:

> The present music employs texts of love between men and women. The songs can be used at occasions of royal banquets, viewing archery, or royal processions outside the court. If these vulgar texts are performed at times when all the government officials are gathered together in front of the court, how can your Majesty retain dignity and respectability? Although I am the *chejo* of the Royal Music Institute I am not well versed in music. According to what I have learned, however, even though *Chinjak* has a vulgar text, it describes a story in which a loyalist is longing for his lord, so that it is quite alright to use the song. But among the texts there are a couple of vulgar ones such as *Hujŏnghwa* and *Manjŏnch'un*. Song texts like *Ch'ihwap'yŏng*, *Pot'aep'yŏng* and *Chŏngdaeŏp*, praising the achievements of the royal ancestors, should be sung so as to applaud the accomplishments of sage kings. Today, female entertainers and musicians would like to omit proper music, playing licentious music. This is extremely bothersome. I desire your Majesty to give an order not to allow the practice of any vulgar songs. (Song B.S. (2) pp.42-3)

One of the so-called 'licentious texts' was 'The Dumpling Shop':
> I went to buy some dumplings at the shop.
> The Muslim master reached out and caught my wrist.
> If word of this is heard outside the shop and spreads around,
> Tarorege tire!
> Naughty little baby dumpling, I'll say it was your talking.
> Te-re-dung-syeng tarire tire!
> Tarire tire tarorege tire!
> Tarore! Now to his bedroom I will also go to sleep.
> Hey, hey! Tarorege tire!
> Tarore! There is no place as dreary as the place we slept.
> (Condit (3), pp.78-9)

Pot'aep'yŏng ('Protecting the Peace') went as follows:
>   The Heavenly mandate's difficult to keep,
>   It prospers but when virtue is achieved.
>   O, august, our noble ancestors!
>   Great, indeed, the mandate they've received.
>
>   The sagely ardour and the wondrous plans
>   Are very bright and very glorious.
>   Fulfilling fate, they open the Great Peace.
>   As utmost goodness leads the black-haired mass.
>
>   They teach and aid all our posterity,
>   Continuing henceforth for ages long.
>   Whatever radiates such a fulsome light
>   'Tis proper thus to praise in hymn and song.   (*ibid.* p. 124)

In addition to Pak Yŏn's restorative work, the 15th century also saw the creation of important new music and the first use of a new mensural notation system (See below, p.62). To speak of 'composition' would scarcely be accurate, and indeed the term 'notation system' gives an exaggerated idea of either its object or its potential. In the 15th century the recognition that music could exist independently of a textual desideratum was only just beginning to gain ground: Apart from military music, all music hitherto had existed simply as the setting of texts, whether religious, poetic or declamatory, and it was the literary message that was all important. The text was written down and could be learned accurately, studied, commented on and elaborated. The music, on the other hand, being of lesser interest, was learned only by imitation and the handing on of oral traditions. Even when notational systems did develop, they were regarded primarily as a kind of simplified aide-memoire, not as a complete description of the way in which music should be performed. It follows from this, first, that the Koreans were not concerned with the derivation of existing music; second, that when music was required to accompany new texts, existing tunes were freely adopted and if necessary adapted; third, that in the process variation and improvisation were both tolerated and encouraged; and last, that it was this process of performance, rather than the deliberate invention of new tunes or an interest in exploiting instrumental possibilities, that led to the evolution of 'new' music (Condit (1)). The most spectacular example of musical creativity was the compilation by order of King Sejong of the suite 'The dragons fly up to heaven'(Lee, P.H.(1)), a long poetic anthology justifying and extolling the deeds of the dynastic ancestors and founders. It was the first demonstration of the newly devised Korean alphabet, *han'gŭl,* promulgated by royal decree in 1446, and to be on the safe side a translation into Chinese characters and a Chinese-style commentary were published with it. The suite was divided into 125 verses of regular length, a feature which the long *kasa* texts abandoned later in the dynasty. The complete musical notation, comprising five settings of the text in

3,345 bars, formed "probably the longest notated piece of music outside the European tradition" (Condit (3) p.26).

In inspiration and execution the work was typical of the growing sense of Korean nationalism, although the music bore witness to the hybrid sentiment of courtly culture. One of its five settings, *Yŏmillak,* took a Chinese tune and elaborated it into a form that was more in keeping with Korean taste. Its title, 'The ruler shares his pleasure with his people', combined praise for the dynasty's founder with a clear reference to the Chinese paragon of political virtue, King Wen of the early Zhou period. It was the only one of the five musical settings that was incomplete, consisting of only five stanzas, but it is the only one that is regularly played today, and as such it is one of several 'metrically expanded' transformations of Chinese into Korean music that still survive (Condit (3)).[9]

On the more academic side of musicology, the late 15th century saw the publication of Sŏng Hyŏn's great musical encyclopoedia *Akhak kwebŏm* ('Standard work of musical studies'), one of the most important achievements to date of Sino-Korean cultural scholarship and yet another example of a 15th century king's personal interest in musical affairs. This time it was King Songjong (1469-1494) who commissioned the work. Though thoroughly Chinese in its structure and approach, and in fact lifting not a little of its material directly from Chinese sources, it guided and dominated all subsequent musical scholarship in Korea, providing practical inspiration even in recent years for such diverse matters as the design for new robes at the National Classical Music Institute and the choreography for the revival of court dances (Lee, H. K. *(6)).*

Dance was an essential component of much musical performance in traditional Korea, whether it was the ritualistic gyrations that accompanied *aak* or the more entertaining but still basically slow and measured dances of *tangak* - which in their turn were still further removed from the lively, uninhibited folk dances of the world outside the court.[10] Chinese dances were introduced to Korea during both the Silla and Koryŏ dynasties, and like the music were designated *tangak.* One of the oldest survivals still performed at the National Classical Music Institute is *P'ogurak* ('Ball-throwing dance'),

Fig. 3
P'ogurak

first seen at the Korean court on 13th December 1073. It is a combination of dance and game, in which two teams of six girls take turns to try and throw a ball through a round hole high up at the top of a model gateway. If they succeed they are given a flower by the 'flower girl'. If they fail, the 'brush girl' paints a black mark on their cheek (fig.3). Whether performed to slow metrical patterns such as *chinyangjo* (in 18:8 time) or *chungmori* (in 12:4) or to a faster one like *kutkori* (in 6:8), the elegant movements of court dance are still capable of creating a sense of controlled excitement. Today, however, it is not only the thrill of perfectly coordinated movement by beautiful girls to the rich texture of Korean orchestral playing that is so uplifting, it is also the shock of realisation that in those gorgeously costumed and coiffured artists lies a direct link with the performing arts of ancient Korea and China, an evocation of entertainment at their courts. History is about people. The historian must endeavour to see the period or subject of his study in terms of the real, emotional people who created and experienced it, to put himself in the place of those for whom his 'history' was simply their daily life, punctuated from time to time by the good or bad fortune of 'historical events'. No people are or ever were more lively than musicians and dancers, and an inherent risk of an academic survey of Korean musical history is that, lacking the biographies of familiar composers and artists such as illuminate the musical life of the West in earlier ages, the emotional meaning of music to people in Korea, whether at court or in the countryside, might be overlooked. Fortunately Korean literature is not short of examples, either of important or of relatively obscure musicians, to counter this danger. Take, for example, this description of court entertainment in 1844:

> The opening over, a young female entertainer *(kisaeng)* with beautiful eyebrows, correcting her hairpin, is ready to sing traditional song:
> Long lyric songs *(kagok)* in *u* and *kyemyŏn* modes – the *soyongi* and *p'yŏllak*;
> Such narrative songs *(kasa)* as *Ch'unmyŏn'gok, Ch'osaga, Ŏbusa, Sangsa pyŏlgok, Hwanggye t'aryŏng,* and *Maehwat'aryŏng*;
> Secular songs *(chapka)* and short lyric songs *(sijo)* – all good to hear.
> Head tied with kerchiefs, female dancers follow the female singer.
> Slow dance is presented along with slow music – the *Sangyŏngsan* and *Chungyŏngsan* of the *Yŏngsan hoesang*.
> Fast dance immediately follows along with the accompaniment of *Seryŏngsan*.[11]
> Oh! A goddess flying down from the Witches Mountain. (Song, B.S. (2) pp.82-3)

It is a powerful jolt to the imagination to observe the timeless beauty of the present-day successors to the royal *kisaeng* at the National Classical Music Institute, so serene, so self-confident, even so haughty in performance, and so lively, high-spirited and girlish off-stage. They evoke the past more effectively than quantities of prose or verse can do, sending a shiver of excitement down the historian's back.[12]

One of the best known of traditional *hyangak* dances is the sword dance *(kŏmgimu* or *kŏmmu)*. Originally a folk dance, it was incorporated into the court repertoire during the Chosŏn dynasty. It commemorates the heroic deed of a teenage boy of Silla, Hwangch'ang, who is said to have used his skill as a sword dancer to enveigle his way into the presence of the enemy king of Paekche before killing him. He was a *hwarang,* a 'flower boy', one of an elite body of highly trained and educated young men dedicated to upholding the honour and ideals of Silla. Despite their elegant dress and use of make-up, these boys were fearsome adversaries. Their training at the Hwarang Academy, based on the Chinese Six Arts and therefore including music, was a Confucian one, but native traditions of shamanism ran strong in Silla and they were well acquainted with its music and ritual. Boys as well as girls were used as dancers at court, and in the early Chosŏn dynasty Confucian moralists even attempted unsuccessfully to have them replace girls altogether. Illustrations from *Chinyŏn ŭigwe* (see below p.203) during the 18th and 19th centuries show the sword dance being performed by four girls (fig.4), but in their hat and dress there is an air of masculinity that serves as a reminder of the semi-military origins of the dance, as well as a similarity with the dress of the shaman.

Fig. 4 The sword dance

舞鼓

Fig. 5 The drum dance

Another popular *hyangak* dance with warlike overtones is the drum dance *(mugo)*. This is believed to date from the 14th century and to have been developed later to celebrate Admiral Yi Sun-sin's victory over Hideyoshi, thereby obtaining its alternative title of 'Victory dance of Ch'ungmu'. A large drum *(kyobanggo)* is set in the middle of the floor on a four-legged frame. In the modern version of the dance it is covered with a brightly coloured silk cloth which initially conceals its true nature, but this does not appear in earlier illustrations (fig.5). Eight dancers circle around it, four holding flowers and four (the principal dancers, *wŏnmu*) drumsticks concealed within their long sleeves. The outer circle, holding their flowers at shoulder height, are the first to approach the drum, which they touch lightly and soundlessly with them. When it is the turn of the *wŏnmu*, they, having lulled the unsuspecting audience into a sense of false security with their apparent gentleness, suddenly bring down their sticks simultaneously and beat the drum with a rousing bang. The advancing and retreating of the two circles symbolizes the movement of military formations, and the dance is reputed to have been used by Admiral Yi to stiffen the morale of his troops during their battles against the Japanese. The two sets of dancers take turns at alternately touching and beating the drum, until the *wŏnmu* execute a long rhythmic sequence and all eight perform a final dance in a circle.

INTRODUCTION

The Japanese wars marked a watershed in the history of the Korean nation. Wholesale destruction of property took place, especially of palaces and works of art, so that any treasures which survive undamaged from before 1592, other than those which have subsequently been recovered from tombs, are unhappily less common than they might have been. The trauma of the invasions threw the Korean people (or at least those who had any reason to ponder upon the country's fortunes and its position in east Asia) into a mental turmoil to which their imminent defeat by the Manchus and the fall of the Ming dynasty only added. The Manchu conquest entailed further destruction and disruption of official life, and though the upper hand among Korean politicians was eventually gained by those who accepted the need to continue to rely on imperial and Confucian bounty - even if it was dispensed temporarily by non-Chinese rulers - some of those with more creative tendencies began to seek solace by developing their artistic skills in less sinicised directions. At court, where envoys from the new rulers in Peking were received, efforts were made to restore *aak,* and for a while it was brought back into use at the Royal Ancestors' Shrine, but it was a real struggle to carry on the duties of the Royal Music Institute at their former level. Books and instruments had been destroyed and many musicians lost. No music at all was played at court between 1637 and 1646. When it was revived, the orchestras were considerably smaller than they had been in the past and it was nearly a hundred years before ritual music was again thought to be satisfactory, even at the Royal Ancestors' Shrine.[13] The ceremonial scenes depicted in the books and on the screens of the 18th and 19th centuries represent the continuation of formal traditions from which much of the originality and sparkle seem to have disappeared. Nevertheless, changes were taking place in the Korean musical repertoire from which entertainment at court benefited. This time, however, it was neither Chinese music nor the coming of envoys from China that instigated them. Instead, new inspiration was being found outside the court, even outside the city, and from the attention which Korean musicians began to pay to their own poetic traditions. Developments in the second half of the dynasty were native in origin, and they were every bit as important as those in the first half that had sought to imitate the Chinese.

Despite the enjoyment which the scholar found in making music for himself, solo music yielded pride of place in Korea to ensemble performance, and has continued to do so even since the development of the *sanjo* form in the 19th century. It was during the second half of the Chosŏn dynasty that there emerged the most famous of all Korean ensemble pieces, an example of chamber music at its most sophisticated that must have matched the pensive and then increasingly self-confident mood of the literati. Its name is *Yŏngsan hoesang* ('Meeting on Spirit Mountain'), and it is still the best loved and most commonly heard item of traditional programme music (fig. 6, Musical Recording 4). In the 15th century it may still have been a simple Buddhist song set to the text of 'Buddha preaching on Spirit Mountain'. Condit ((3) p.101) translates it as follows:

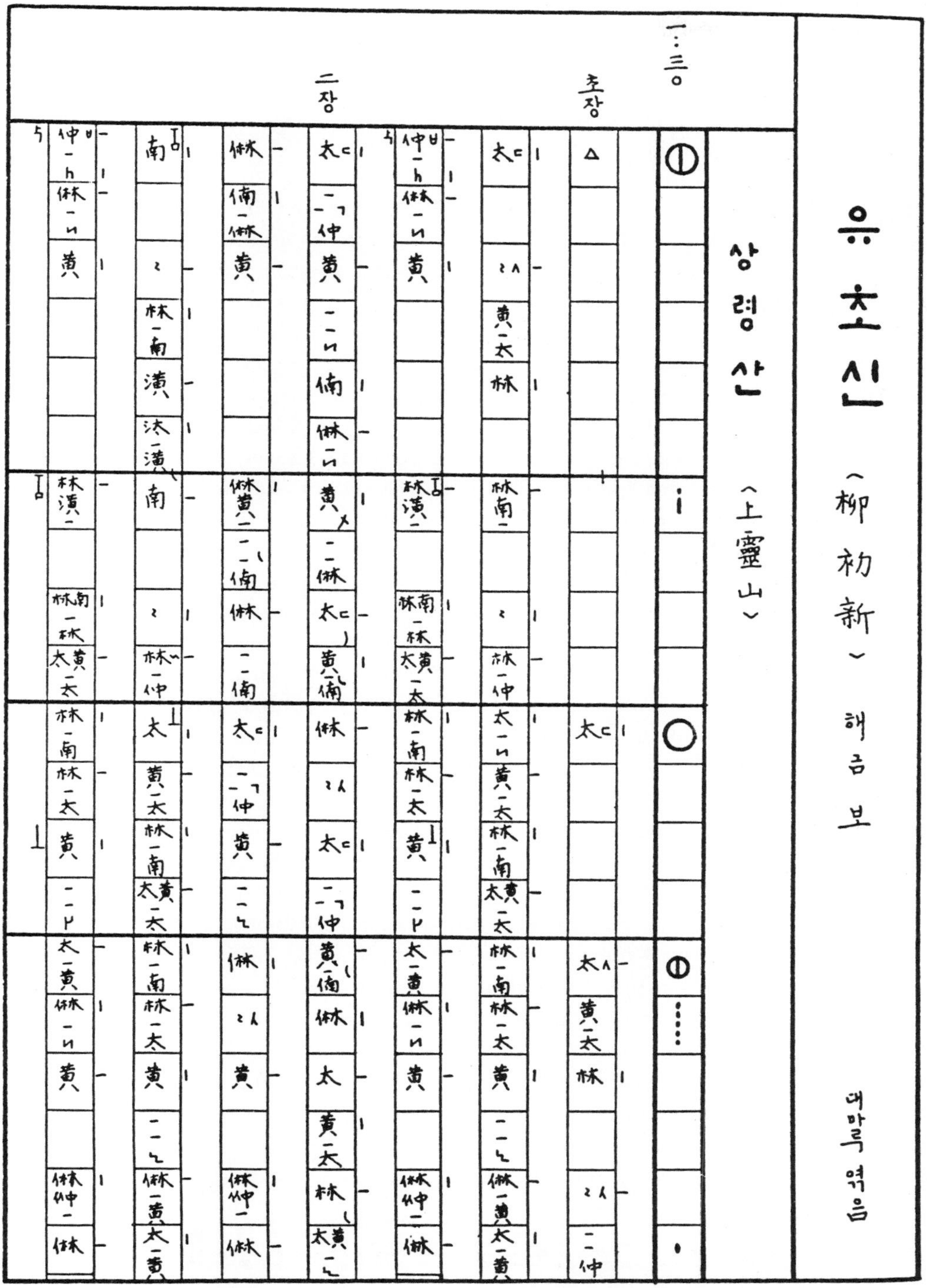

Fig. 6 Page from a modern Korean score for the *haegŭm* part for
Yŏngsan hoesang

45

INTRODUCTION

Buddha taught at Vulture Peak.
Song of endless life.
Gods ride wisps of purple smoke,
Dancing by th'embroidered screen.
Flow'r-bedecked they slowly turn:
Long life for our King and Queen.

By the 17th century the words had been dropped and its elaboration into an orchestral suite had begun. Today it exists in three main versions, one consisting of nine movements for strings and soft winds (*kŏmun'go, kayagŭm, yanggŭm, haegŭm, p'iri, taegŭm, tanso* and *changgo*), one of eight movements for a wind ensemble known as *samhyŏn yukkak,* and one of eight movements for an ensemble of strings and loud winds (*kŏmun'go, kayagŭm, yanggŭm, haegŭm, ajaeng, p'iri, taegŭm, tangjŏk, changgo* and *chwago*).[14] Each version has more than one name of its own, the first being the one commonly referred to as [*Hyŏnak*] *Yŏngsan* but also called *Kŏmun'go hoesang* or *Chunggwang jigok,* the second known as *Kwanak Yŏngsan hoesang, Samhyŏn Yŏngsan hoesang* or *T'aep'ungnyu,* and the third being either *P'yongjo hoesang* or *Yuch'osinjigok.* A complete playing of all nine sections lasts nearly one hour but a selection from the music is often made, and individual sections are to be heard in many other contexts. The suite only assumed its present form in the 19th century and the origins of the component sections are unknown. The first four seem to be related, perhaps in the form of variations, and may be derived from a Buddhist chant of the 15th century or earlier (Musical Example 3), while number seven bears the title *Yŏmbul,* 'Praying to Buddha'. These five at least show some link with the original nature of the text. Other movements include popular dance tunes and the final one, *Kunak* or 'Military music', clearly stems from a different milieu and is even in a different key from the remainder. Like the *sanjo,* the suite is performed without a break between the movements, beginning slowly and increasing in speed so that, in the words of Lee Hye-Ku, the piece "begins with dignity and ends with humour."[15] If its origins were not in the court, *Yŏngsan hoesang* was nevertheless favoured by the upper classes and conveys all the qualities of the Confucian gentry, balance, refinement, consideration, reliability, and the control of emotions. It is what the Koreans call *chŏngak,* 'proper' or 'upright music'. But the upper classes were only a tiny fraction of the deeply divided Chosŏn society. Their way of life was quite different from that of ordinary people, whose behaviour lacked much of the sophistication and restraint with which Confucian education endowed their leaders, and whose culture was less inhibited and more vibrant. They might well have found a complete performance of *Yŏngsan hoesang* hard to appreciate. However, sections of it were played separately to accompany court dances, such as the crane dance, and it is not unlikely that the comings and goings of court musicians and

Musical Example 3. A reconstruction of the original chant for *Yŏngsan hoesang*

dancers would help to spread some of the tunes across, or back into, the countryside. The year 1634 may have been a critical one in this process. Hitherto, court entertainment had included a mixture of plays, acrobatics and dances, some of which dated from the Silla and Koryŏ periods and were now incompatible with the moral outlook of the Confucian leadership. In 1634 King Injo banished *sandae* masked dance plays from court, and the professional slave-actors who performed them and who had lived outside the walls of the capital dispersed into the provinces, thereby encouraging the development of regional masked dance dramas of which many still exist today. Music does not play a major part in these dramas: Social satire and attacks on the aristocracy and dissolute Buddhist clergy, wrapped up in comic and often exceedingly crude situations, provide the principal if unvarying attraction. The band usually consists at the maximum of *p'iri*, *taegŭm*, *haegŭm*, *kkwaenggwari*, *changgo* and *puk*, and although the music has sometimes been dismissed as trivial, it may be significant that two of the favourite rhythms encountered in the masked dances are *yŏmbul* and *t'aryŏng*, a slow 6-beat and a moderate 12:8 beat both of which occur in sections of *Yŏngsan hoesang*, and that *Samhyŏn Yŏngsan hoesang* itself is used to accompany parts of the best known of all *sandae* dramas, that from Yangju in Kyŏnggi Province (Lee D.H.(1) p.147).

For their part the gentry were unlikely to ignore and quite likely to enjoy folk music (*minsogak*). Unlike *aak* and *tangak* it was part of their native inheritance, and however sinicised they purported to be they were first and foremost Korean. They knew the lullabies, they probably heard the work-songs of tenant farmers in their fields and their bands at times of celebration such as Ch'usŏk, they were entertained with folk music from troupes of both local and itinerant players, and even the royal family attended religious functions at which the music incorporated folk music. There was music everywhere, and most of the folk music of today, as well as the 'proper music' that is still heard in the concert halls, dates from the Chosŏn dynasty.

The contrast between *chŏngak* and *minsogak* is apparent if we compare *Yŏngsan hoesang* with an instrumental piece of folk music, *Sinawi* (Musical Recording 5). *Sinawi*, like *Yŏngsan hoesang*, begins slowly and builds up to a climax. Its ensemble may include the *kŏmun'go*, *kayagŭm*, *ajaeng*, *p'iri*, *taegŭm*, *haegŭm*, and perhaps the *t'aep'yŏngso*, and percussion instruments drawn from the *changgo*, *puk*, *ching* (large gong), *kkwaenggwari* (small gong) and *para* (cymbals). The players have opportunities between the ensemble passages for solo extemporization rather as they do in western jazz, in which each player can display his skill in a free and melodic way which is quite different from the precision of *Yŏngsan hoesang*. The result is a performance that brims over with energy and passion, more evocative of the market place than the audience chamber, or perhaps of the shaman ceremony from which it is thought to have been derived. *Sinawi*, in its turn, may have been one of the sources of inspiration for *sanjo*, both of them originating in the south-western province of Chŏlla.

Another striking illustration of the cultural dichotomy of the class system is encoun-

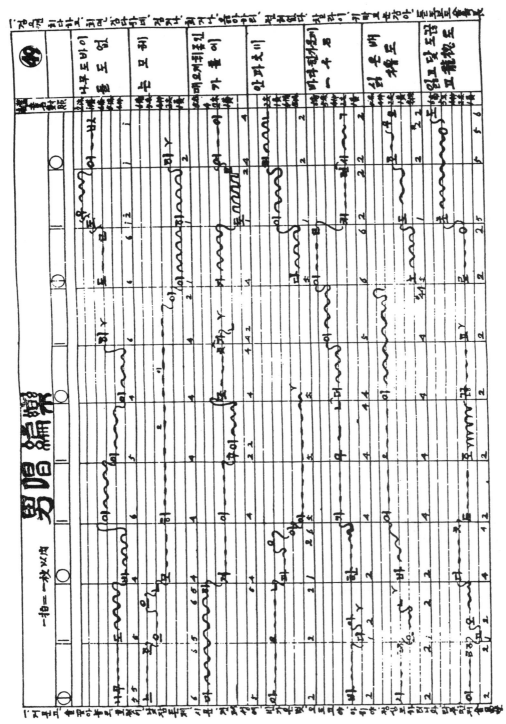

Fig. 7 Modern singing – school notation of *p'yŏllak*, a piece of Korean *kagok*

tered in vocal music. The song forms of *chŏngak* consist of the long narrative song, *kasa,* the lyric song *kagok,* and the short lyric song *sijo* (Chang (3)). All three are extremely difficult to perform and almost as difficult to appreciate, and in all three the technique demanded of the singer is of as much importance as the text or the melody. The music is slow, ranges in pitch from the very low to falsetto, and follows a melismatic line in which the relationship between the rhythm and the line of text is not immediately evident: *kasa,* for example, usually consists of seven or eight syllables per line, each line being set to two groups of five or six beats. Since a stanza normally contains a regular four lines this may not be too difficult to grasp, but in *kagok* the five lines of the stanza are of irregular length, the beat may be arranged in groups of five and eleven or three and seven, depending on the speed of the song (eleven beats representing three syllables of text), and whilst a word which requires emphasis may be of quite short duration, the second syllable of a less important word or the Korean post-positional indicators may follow a long-drawn out melismatic sequence (fig. 7, Musical Recording 7). Lee Hye-Ku illustrates this quite clearly in the following analysis:

1. *Tongch'ang i-/palgat nŭnya-*
2. *Nogojil i-/ujijinda-*
3. *So ch'inun ahae nom ŭn-/sangi ani irŏtnŭnya.*
4. *Chae nŏmŏ-*
5. *Sare kin patŭl-/ŏnje kalyŏ-/hanŭni.*

The eastern window grows light
and skylarks are singing.
Is the boy who fodders the ox
still not out?
When will the long field
over the ridge be ploughed?   (tr. D. McCann)

The corresponding beat pattern is as follows:
1. 11 beats/21 beats (5.11.5)
2. 11/16 (5.11)
3. 16 (5.11)/21 (5.11.5)
Interlude: 16 beats (11.5)
4. 27 (11.5.11)
5. 16 (5.11)/16 (5.11)/16 (5.11)
Postlude: 53 beats (5.11.5.11.5.11.5) (Lee H.K. (4), p.8)

The verse form now known as *sijo,* dating back as far as the Silla dynasty, has just three lines to the stanza and its musical settings, which originated in the 18th century, are correspondingly simpler than *kagok.* Once again it is exceedingly slow, usually accompanied only by the *changgo* instead of the small ensemble which usually accompanies *kagok,* and whilst the latter may be composed of one of two modes using a pentatonic scale, the basic *sijo* melody has only one mode, and what is more, is based on only three notes, A^b, B^b and E^b (Musical Recording 8).

> Music is often considered to have three basic elements: rhythm, melody and harmony. *Sijo,* of course, lacks harmony in the usual sense; its rhythm is open to some doubt; and its melody is quite simple. What, then, are the important constituents of *sijo* performance?

> Long ago, when I was in college preparatory school, I went one day to a grove of pine trees and lay down on the ground. I had not meditated for long before my imagination was filled with wild fancies; to this day I remember clearly the impression made by the sound of the wind blowing through the pines, like a heavenly music. Blowing in the pine groves over my head, the wind rushed by in a crescendo, followed by a decrescendo as the wind died away; after straining, the pine needles shook back in a kind of tremolo, giving a very settling sound. The delicate variations in sound made by the pine trees varied with the force of the wind blowing in and passing out.

> The long, drawn-out sounds of the wind blowing through the pine grove could hardly be said to have melody or rhythm; what gave the sense of beauty could only be the dynamics, that is, the changes in power. Like the wind in the pines, *sijo* has no harmony, little rhythm, and a simple melody; the sense of pleasure in hearing *sijo* is aroused by the variation in dynamics. (Lee H.K.(7) p.157)

Meditation of a different kind belonged, and still does, to the Buddhist temple, where music is associated with the rites immediately preceding and following death. Both texts and rites were first introduced from China and it seems likely that by the Silla period chant was already a mixture of Chinese and native music. Today, Chinese or Sanskrit texts are sung to *pŏmp'ae,* shorter, simpler passages to the style known as *hossori,* more elaborate ones to *chissori.* Trained singers are required for both, but because of their length and the difficulty of their melismatic passages and dynamic range – from the barely audible to the very loud – those pieces which are still performed

Musical Example 4.
Hwach'ŏng

from the *chissori* repertoire are diminishing. The fact that their texts are drawn from Chinese prose or from Sanskrit helps to account for the longer sweeps of their melodic lines, in contrast to the more regular patterns encountered in *hossori*, which is the setting of 5- or 7-syllabled Chinese verse. Chants in the *hossori* repertoire are more common. Texts in the Korean language are sung to *yŏmbul*, a much simpler style of chant which includes long passages of recitative, and in a derivative from *yŏmbul*, *hwach'ŏng* (Musical Example 4, Musical Recording 9). John Levy notes the similarity between *hwach'ŏng* and some Korean folk songs.[16] Hahn Man-young has also pointed out that the main tri-tonal emphasis in *pŏmp'ae,* of a fourth and a minor third (C♯-F♯-A) is the same as that of the eastern folk song region. He has drawn attention to the origins of *Yŏngsan hoesang* in Buddhist chant and to a possible connection between the vocal techniques required in chant and those of *kagok* (Hahn (1) p.161). The musical influence of Buddhist chant may therefore have been more widespread in the past than its limited appreciation today might suggest, and in view of the strength of Buddhism at all social levels this would not be surprising.

Chant is usually accompanied by beats on the *mokt'ak*, 'wooden fish', a block of wood carved with a single slit and painted with the eyes of a fish, the symbol of ever-watchful wakefulness. Itinerant monks might beg alms by singing *hwach'ŏng* and accompanying themselves on the *puk* (drum) and the *kkwaenggwari* (small gong). Despite the range of instruments professed by the Buddhist angels, the devas, melodic instruments today are only used for the accompaniment of three well-known Buddhist dances, and there is no firm evidence that the situation was ever any different. The three dances are the cymbal dance (*parach'um*), the butterfly dance (*nabich'um*), and the drum dance (*popkoch'um*), and the 'orchestra' may consist of *t'aep'yŏngso, para* (large cymbals), *nabal* (straight trumpet), *sora* (conch shell), *mokt'ak* and *puk*. They are danced to chants whose purpose is to prepare for or to celebrate death and the release of the soul into paradise. Taking part in a liturgical rite, therefore, the monks dedicate their performance to Buddha, and only on the stage do lay artists seek to draw attention to themselves as polished and graceful performers.

Korea has a large corpus of folk songs with as much variety of tempo, mood and subject matter as any other part of the world. They include work songs, love songs, games songs, religious songs. They are happy, sad, resigned, discontented, humorous. They are fast and passionate, slow and reflective. Historical sources reveal the titles and some of the words of folk songs from as far back as the Three Kingdoms and United Silla periods. Although no tunes of such antiquity have survived, a hint of early origins is given by some of those that share features with Buddhist chant. Their most common rhythmic patterns are *chungmori* (moderate 12:4), *t'aryŏng* (a faster 12:8) and *chinyangjo* (a slow 6 beats), but if the beat is comparatively simple a complication is introduced by the rules governing the choice of words, which are repeated according to fixed patterns. The refrain, often sung by the chorus in answer to the soloist's verse, may include nonsense syllables. Some figured amongst the songs used by the *kŏllip'ae* or *norip'ae*, itinerant entertainment troupes whose female members specialised in singing and dance. These troupes were responsible for spreading polished versions of the best songs, known as *chapka*, beyond the local limits of some of the specialised work songs. People in all regions, for example, could appreciate a rice-planting or a weeding song (Musical Example 5), whereas the songs sung by the pearl-diving fisherwomen of Cheju Island would be of little interest outside their own community.

Musical Example 5. Rice planting song of South Chŏlla province

Agricultural tasks constituted the most frequent subjects of work songs. However, the category of music known as farmers' music (*nongak*) covered more than just the accompaniment of these occupational songs, and was indispensable at the celebration of social and religious events such as the New Year, Buddha's birthday, and the autumn festival of Ch'usŏk. Sometimes the performances were given by the *kŏllip'ae*, sometimes by local bands drawn from the menfolk of the community. These naturally featured regional variations of style, some of which still exist, but it is nevertheless possible to describe a 'standard' processional band of today, which though it may no longer accompany the shaman around the village as it used to do, still occasionally winds its way through the streets towards the entertainment ground, gathering spectators as it goes. At its head come the banners, one of them perhaps tipped with pheasants' feathers and to be used later as part of the performance, held against the lower torso in what may once have been a fertility rite. Leading the band itself are two wind instruments, the *nabal* and the *t'aep'yŏngso*, neither of which is important in this context even though the latter is the only melodic instrument present. The first of the percussionists come next, the *kkwaenggwari*, one of whom is the leader of the band (*sangsoe*). The *kkwaenggwari* is a small gong struck with a wooden hammer, and with it the *sangsoe* beats out the processional dance rhythms, switching bewilderingly backwards and forwards between compound subdivisions of the basic twelve-beat structure. Following in the swaying line are the smaller gongs, *ching,* and the drums, *changgo, puk,* and the small hand drum *sogo.* Some of the players may have long streamers attached to their hats, which they flick and twirl in a wide radius around them with amazing control of the neck muscles, an art which, it has been suggested, may be derived from ancient battle-ground manoeuvres. The *kkwaenggwaris'* hats, tipped with feathers, may also point to a military origin, whilst the bright paper chrysanthemums which adorn the hats of the rest of the band may be traced right back to Silla, and Buddhist origins. Bringing up the rear of the procession dance the *chapsaek,* mimics, actors, comics and entertainers of all sorts, cracking jokes with the onlookers and advertising the coming display. Performing troupes which show off individual skills are said to emphasize the religious element in farmers' music, while those that perform mainly in groups may be a reminder that farmers might sometimes find themselves caught up in battle-ground situations. There is no doubt, however, that the hope most frequently uppermost in their minds, season by season, was that the spirits would bless their crops: Fertility rites and music have probably had as long an association in Korea as elsewhere in the world.

The central figure in the essential and regular routine of communicating with the spirits, a figure, like the military commander, to inspire awe and not a little fear but one whose advent promised advantages rather than the inevitable disasters of war, was the shaman. The shaman was generally female and was in a position to exercise great authority in the community. Her powers were invoked by all from king to commoner. She officiated at national ceremonies such as the Koryŏ dynasty's *P'algwanhoe* festival,[17] and even the strong Confucian ethics of the early Chosŏn, disparaging shamanism as low-class superstition, failed to drive her permanently out of the circles of either provincial or central government. During the reign of King Sejong she and her family were employed as musicians at court. She visited the homes of humble villagers to drive out the spirits of sickness, summon and placate the spirits of the ancestors, and seek peace and favours for the coming year. The ritual and chants used by the shaman often borrowed from the music and even the pantheon of Buddhism and Chinese popular religion. Condit (3), for example, quotes a 15th century shamanist song in which the four Buddhist Guardian Kings (*Sach'ŏnwang*) are praised:

> In the East, upright sky-king lord, hail !
> In the South, wide-eyed sky-son sky-king lord, hail !
> Namu in the West, spread-out sky-king lord, hail !
> The North mountain-side Vaisravan sky-king lord, hail !
> Tarire tarori romaha,
> Tireng tiri tairire romaha,
> Toram tarire taroring tireri,
> Tarireng tireri.
> Within, without, yellow four-eyed sky-king lord, hail !   (pp.82-4)

In another song, a Chinese deity of the Koryŏ period is invoked:
> Will you cure sickness, Three-wall Great King ?
> Will you cure trouble, Three-wall Great King ?
> Sickness and trouble harrass us here,
> Please drive it all away now.
> Tarong tari, Three-wall Great King,
> Tarong tari, Three-wall Great King,
> Please always care for us.   (*Ibid.* pp.88-89)

INTRODUCTION

The stages of the seance, or *kut,* were much the same everywhere and were not unlike those which took place in the very different atmosphere of the Confucian shrine: After the calling down of the spirits came the offering of food and drink (and in modern shaman rites money and cigarettes), the presentation of the supplicants' wishes or enquiries and the awaiting of a response, and finally the farewell. The music of this emotional experience was a kind of *sinawi,* less structured indeed than the *sinawi* performed in the modern concert hall but with a haunting, wailing sound that must have been familiar to one and all in town and country. Nowadays farmers' music has become separated from shamanist ritual, which is normally accompanied by a *p'iri,* perhaps a *haegŭm* and a *taegŭm* as well, and two or three percussion instruments, but in the past there was considerable interchange between the two and the shaman's husband was probably one of her accompanists as well as a member of the farmers' band. The shaman herself used a *changgo* in the course of her performance. The musicians accompanied her chant and dances and perhaps performed on their own between sections of the ritual. Dance was an important feature of the ceremony. Some of the dance tunes were borrowed from Buddhist and folk dances (Huhm (1) p.27), and grew faster and faster until the shaman was induced to enter an exhausted trance, when she was believed to be in communion with the spirits who had entered her body. The build-up of tension and the explosion of frenetic energy, culminating in a sudden, anti-climactic ending, is recalled by the closing stages of the *kayagŭm sanjo* and the trance-like state of its performer. A *kut* might last for hours or for days. Not only were incantations made to the spirits, but the opportunity was also seized for teaching the supplicants about the spirits and their magical powers. The recitative might therefore include the elements of a story containing history, philosophy, natural

Musical Example 6. Shamanistic song from the Seoul area : *Norae Karak* for *Sak Sanmanura Kori*

science, and undoubtedly romance. It was from this that the link with the dramatic story-telling form, *p'ansori,* was forged in the second half of the Chosŏn dynasty.

After assisting the shaman in her rites and reaching the entertainment ground, the farmers' band then accompanied some of the forms of relaxation that provided welcome relief from the monotony and problems of peasant life. Dances, games, tug-of-war and tight-rope walking were all popular, as were masked dance dramas. Most of these still feature in rural entertainments today. The extant masked dance dramas can be classified into three groups:

Sŏnang ('Guardian spirit') ritual plays. These were part of the seasonal country rites which formed a consecutive series of events, including farmers' music and dance and rites at the spirit shrine, and in which exorcism was important.

Sandae togam plays. In the early Chosŏn dynasty these were managed by a government office of the same name, and following their banning at court in 1634 they eventually came to be associated with urban centres in the provinces. Variant forms of these plays were known as *ogwangdae* ('five actors') and *yayu* ('field plays'). They too were preceded by sacrifices to the spirits, and the themes of their scenes, their principal characters, and the colour and style of their masks were much the same as those in the *sŏnang* group.

Sajagye ('Lion mask plays'). The history of the lion mask plays and dances is very ancient. It can be traced to China, where the lion was worshipped as a bodhisattva, and to other parts of central and south Asia. It had appeared in Korea by the Silla dynasty and from there crossed over to Japan. The Korean lion was believed to be capable of driving evil spirits out of households as the procession wound its way round the village prior to the beginning of the play. Apart from the scenes in which the lion dances (to *t'aryŏng* or *kutkŏri* rhythms), eats his rival the *tambo,* and is cured of his subsequent indigestion not by the vain efforts of the Buddhist monk but by the more mundane treatment afforded by the apothecary, the topics that make up *sajagye* are again similar to those of *sŏnang* plays. Masked dramas have no story line or plot running through them: Except for the recurrent appearance of the main characters their scenes are independent of each other and the best known incidents or situations-such as the seduction of the aristocrat's wife by the dissolute monk-may occur in plays belonging to any or all of the three groups. We have already observed that the music used to accompany masked plays was neither distinctive nor particularly important, though of course without the rhythm of the dance even the powerful and emotional message of the social satire would have been seriously weakened. Their polemics aside, the special interest of masked dance dramas lies in the full range of their characterisation and an analysis of the masks themselves, subjects which apart from the note appended to plate 41 lie beyond the scope of this book.[18] It is worth reiterating, however, that music and rhythm were ubiquitous in traditional Korea. Regardless of their technical merit, their psychological release value to the farmers was essential, and without them no outdoor entertainment would have been complete.

One form of entertainment that did not develop in Korea, despite its popularity in China, was the opera. *P'ansori*, which probably stemmed from the recitative of the shaman and the public story-teller, was its nearest equivalent. Originally the telling of the tale may have been interspersed by dramatic scenes played by the entertainment troupe, but gradually these sections disappeared until the story-teller was left to indicate the action simply by gesture and the use of his only props, a fan and a handkerchief. The beginnings of *p'ansori* may lie in south-west Korea somewhere back in the early Chosŏn period, and by the time of its greatest development in the later part of the dynasty it was popular even at court. The text used there was based on Chinese stories and was less vulgar, and less amusing, than those performed in the villages. Today only five stories remain in the entire *p'ansori* repertoire. A complete performance of just one could take up to eight hours, but such a test of stamina for either the singer or the audience is rarely attempted, and shortened versions are much more common. The singer is accompanied by a single drummer with a *puk*, who utters cries of encouragement during the sung sections of the story and engages in repartee during the passages of speech (Musical Recording 11). The audience may also join in with the backchat as well, as they certainly would have done on the entertainment ground in earlier times. Long outdoor performances may have something to do with the harsh and unnatural style of voice production required of the *p'ansori* singer, which demands long training and great physical stamina, yet since the late 19th century women as well as men have been successful performers, and a singer may not reach the peak of his or her career until his early fifties (Lee, B.H.(1)(3)).

In addition to the two most common Korean modes, *u* and *kyemyŏn*, five others may be heard in *p'ansori*.[19] Each of the seven is used to suggest characterisation, mood or occasion : *U* for example, the mode of the male character, implies calmness and authority; *kyemyŏn*, the feminine mode, sadness; *p'yŏng*, cheerfulness; *kyŏng*, the feeling of sophistication associated with the capital Seoul ; *sŏllŏngje*, the loudness of soldiers or official attendants; *sŏkhwa*, the playing of the *kayagŭm; menari*, the tunes of Kyŏngsang Province. Rhythmic pattern also varies according to the stages and mood of the narrative. For example the slowest, *chinyang*, consists of a cycle in phrases of six beats and accompanies the recital of slow or sad events. By contrast *chungjungmori*, a moderately fast 12 : 8 pattern, is used to describe happy occasions. Another 12 : 8 pattern, *chajinmori*, occurs at moments of tension, while *ŏnmori*, a fast, irregular pattern in 10 : 8, gives a sense of mystery.

In *p'ansori*, as in *nongak* and *sanjo*, the large number of rhythmic variations indicates the high level of musical sophistication to be found at the entertainment ground of the Korean village by the 19th century. All three of these forms are still popular today, and no kind of traditional instrumental music is more commonly studied than the *sanjo*. Like *Yŏngsan hoesang* and *sinawi*, the *sanjo* is a suite of continuous movements which begin slowly and increase in speed and rhythmic complexity. It is for single instrument with *changgo* accompaniment. *Sanjo* means 'scattered tunes', for it grew out of the joining together of folk tunes. Like other forms of folk music *sanjo* was not written down but learned by the imitation of a master, so that schools developed in the style of, for example, Kim Ch'ang-jo (1865-1920), and the personal *sanjo* of the great performers were preserved. Only after a pupil had himself become outstandingly proficient might he branch out into the formation of his own *sanjo*, which would probably be a clear derivative from that of his teacher. The total number of *sanjo* extant for any particular instrument remains limited: For the *kayagŭm*, which is the most frequently employed *sanjo* instrument, less than ten are in popular use, and the nearest that any artist in modern times has come to creating a new *sanjo* distinctive enough to bear his own name may be heard in the variations that Hwang Byungki has introduced into the *sanjo* of Kim Yun-dŏk.

The performance of all six possible movements in a *sanjo* may take up to one hour. The minimum number that can be played is three (in slow, medium and fast time), but the player may decide exactly how many to include when he senses the mood of his audience, and his accompanist will be familiar enough with his style to be able to follow his lead. He begins with a free rhythmic tuning section before moving into the first movement, a slow six beats (*chinyang*, $\rfloor$. = 35). Here his ability to control the dying strains of each string as it is plucked, binding together the notes with imperceptible melismatic bonds, is the first true test of his musicianship. The next movement is in a moderate 12 beat pattern, *chungmori* ($\rfloor$. = 84-92), and is followed by one with four beats in a triple subdivision, *chungjungmori* ($\rfloor$. = 80-96). *Chajinmori* is a faster movement in the same rhythm ($\rfloor$. = 96-144), and finally, in *tanmori* ($\rfloor$. = 208-230), virtuosity of a different kind is called for. The tempo is now a rapid four beats with duple subdivision, which the drummer maintains with a far from simple vocabulary of his own while the soloist weaves intricate melodic and rhythmic patterns around him (Musical Recording 12). Thus the *sanjo* player ends by whole-heartedly embracing the duple rhythm common in Korean folk song, on which his piece is based. Rhythmic pattern in folk song frequently favours a duple compound structure, 6 : 8 or 12 : 8, and less frequently a triple compound 9 : 8, yet Korea alone amongst the musical nations of East Asia shows a marked interest in triple meter, and by the end of the Chosŏn dynasty had already perhaps investigated the science of rhythm more thoroughly than any other country in the world. In common with many other parts of the world, however, it does not make a feature of harmony, attention being focussed instead upon the melodic line and its ornamentation, the tone colour achieved by the combination of different instruments, and the intricate complexities of rhythm. Wide vibrato is prominent in the performance of both court and folk music on the plucked and bowed strings, the wind instruments, and in the vocal forms. In instrumental music it is most noticeable in slow movements, such as *chinyang*.

Rhythmic patterns, known as *changdan*, are usually announced by the two hands of the *changgo* player and may identify the movements by name, as they do in *sanjo*. They do not, as in the manner of western terms such as *largo, presto, scherzo* or *minuetto*, refer exclusively either to tempo or to meter, but to a combination of these and other characteristics. The *changdan* occur in short recurrent phrases, easily memorable and recognizable (fig.8) The main features of the six principal ones are as follows:

1. Chinyang
   (i) lasts approximately 10 seconds ;
   (ii) appears in very slow passages ;
   (iii) is usually in multiples of six beats (e.g. 18:8) ;
   (iv) becomes more active towards the end.

2. Chungmori
   (i) lasts approximately 10 seconds;
   (ii) appears in passages of moderate speed;
   (iii) is usually in 12:4 time;
   (iv) emphasizes the first and ninth beats.

3. Chungjungmori
   (i) lasts approximately 3-4 seconds;
   (ii) has a swinging dance rhythm;
   (iii) tends towards duple rhythm, though the meter sometimes swings to-wards a triple rhythm (e.g. 2×6:8, 3:4+6:8 etc.);
   (iv) puts emphasis on the first and briefly just before the fourth beats.

4. Kutkōri (interchangeable with *chungjungmori*)
   (i) lasts approximately 3-4 seconds;
   (ii) has a swinging dance rhythm;
   (iii) tends towards duple or quadruple rhythm (e.g. 2×6:8).

5. Chajinmori
   (i) is slightly shorter in duration than *chungjungmori*;
   (ii) is the commonest pattern in so-called 'fast' music (but cf. the speed of *tanmori* below!)
   (iii) prefers, like *chungjungmori,* mainly quadruple rhythm, though the meter often changes;
   (iv) puts emphasis on the first and briefly just before the fourth beats.

6. Tanmori
   (i) is the shortest classical pattern;
   (ii) occurs in very fast passages of music;
   (iii) is in quadruple rhythm;
   (iv) has emphasis on the first beat.   (Provine (3) pp.156-175)

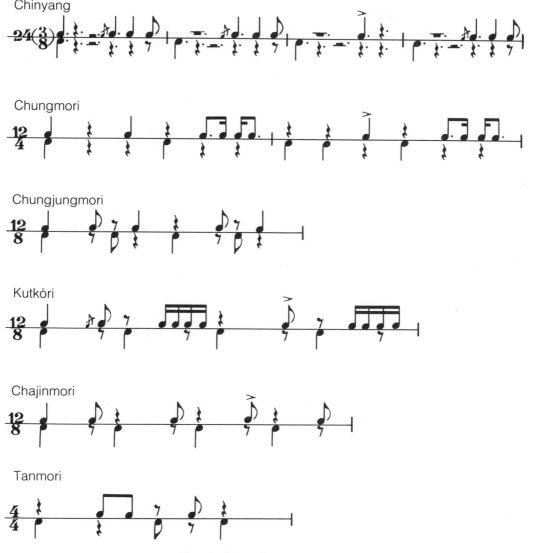

Fig. 8 *Changdan* patterns

None of the notational systems used in Korea before the adoption of staff notation in very recent years was adequate for the transcription of any kind of music, whether court or folk, and at the complexities of *p'ansori* and *sanjo* no attempt was even made. Notation made a comparatively late appearance in Korea, and when its need was finally and incontrovertibly recognised in the 15th century a confusing variety of systems evolved (Lee H.K.(7) pp.23-42). Different types of music were notated in different ways, the *kŏmun'go* having a system of its own derived from that of the *guqin* in China. Three systems were introduced from China, one of which, *yulchabo,* was the most suitable for transcribing *aak,* in which all notes were of equal value. It is still in

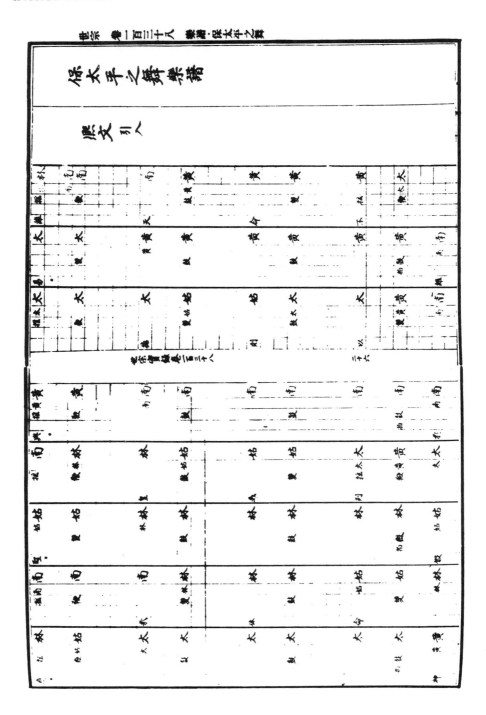

Fig. 9 Passages from two *chŏngganbo* transcriptions of *Pot'aep'yŏng*,

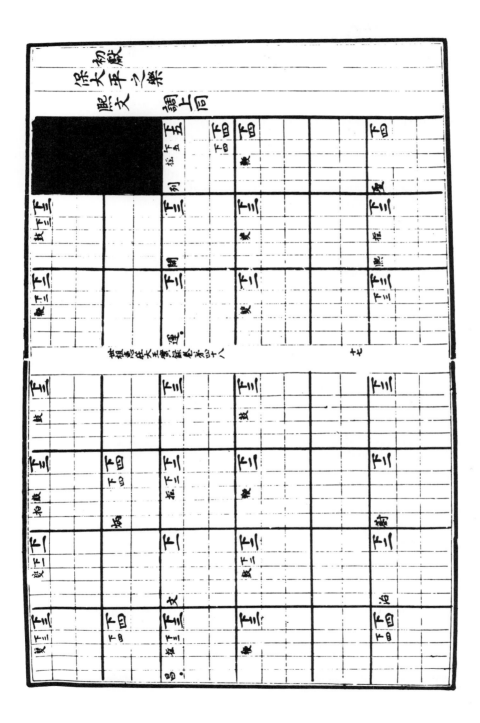

(p.60) in King Sejong's version, (p.61) in King Sejo's version

use today. However, it was only the Korean system of *chŏngganbo,* developed during the reign of King Sejong and improved under his son Sejo, that was able to indicate both pitch and rhythm (fig.9). The score consists of a linear matrix on which the notes are entered from top to bottom, right to left. One line normally contains 16 squares, each representing one beat. Pitches are shown by symbols chosen from one of the other notational systems, in most cases Chinese characters representing the five notes of the pentatonic scale. To these were added further marks indicating ornamentation, accompanying drum-beats, etc. (Condit (4)). The system does not, however, indicate tempo, and we are reminded not only that in earlier times the nature of performance was not as fixed as it is today, but also that primary importance was attached to the information imparted by the teacher, whose skill rendered written music all but unnecessary. The combination of these two factors – incomplete notation and the crucial role of the teacher – may have contributed to the decline of traditional music in the early part of the 20th century, when with little official encouragement and growing competition from western music it became increasingly unfamiliar to most Koreans. Happily, however, its roots proved to be as deep as those of Korean nationalism and its traditions as widespread as the branches of the *ginko* tree. Under the newly established Music Department court music and dance survived both the disappearance of the royal court itself in 1910 and the Japanese occupation. In 1951 the Music Department was succeeded by the National Classical Music Institute. This famous institution now spearheads the revival of traditional music through the work of its high school, the research of its scholars, and the training and frequent performances of its musicians and dancers, whose complement was increased five-fold in the ten years between 1974 and 1984. At the same time the number of universities at which Korean music may be studied has grown by about the same amount, and concerts of tradition-al music are well attended in city and university auditoria. The repertoire of the Seoul City Traditional Orchestra extends beyond the complete range of classical pieces – which even allowing for the inclusion of *sanjo* and the various vocal forms is comparatively limited by western standards – and embraces new works for Korean instruments. The best known of contemporary Korean composers is Hwang Byungki, whose brilliant writing for the *kayagŭm* stretches the descriptive power of the instru-ment far beyond anything that could have been foreseen earlier in the century. Yet for all his use of new fingering techniques, his expanded vocabulary of musical phraseolo-gy and effects, and his imaginative choice of subject matter, much of Hwang's work is clearly rooted in his Korean musical inheritance. So are other modern compositions such as the setting of sections of *p'ansori* to full orchestral accompaniment. Others are more frankly experimental, exploring rhythmic possibilities even with the *ŏ,* the *ch'uk* and the *mokt'ak,* reviving the dwindling fortunes of the *p'yŏnjong, saenghwang* and *hun,* and attempting to combine the forces of both Korean and western orchestras. Thus, both in the visible and tangible form of its instruments and in the manner of its performance, the continuity of Korean music has been safely maintained and is being given every opportunity to flourish anew.

3. Korean Instruments

With few exceptions, the instruments played in Korea today are drawn from the range of those known in China from the Han dynasty onwards. Some, like the *saenghwang*, have remained basically unchanged for two thousand years and may still be heard in both countries. A small but significant group have survived in more regular use in Korea than anywhere else : These include the most important Chinese ritual instruments the bells *(p'yŏnjong)* and chimes *(p'yŏn'gyŏng),* as well as the *ajaeng* and some of the more colourful percussion instruments. The *kŏmun'go* has developed unique Korean characteristics which now separate it from its relatives of Chinese ancestry. The *pip'a* (Ch. *pipa*), still beloved by the Chinese, has been abandoned by the Koreans, whilst the *konghu* harp has disappeared from use throughout the Far East.

Extant examples of Korean instruments dating from more than a hundred or so years ago are exceedingly rare. Unlike those in China, Korean tombs have not so far yielded any recognisable musical instruments among their treasures. The reasons for this striking lacuna are a matter for conjecture. The bells and chimes, which are amongst the most ancient and the most durable survivals in the tombs of the Shang and Zhou nobility, were not officially presented to the Korean court until 1116 A.D. By that time they and other instruments had ceased to be placed even in Chinese tombs. They may have been known in Korea at an earlier date but there is nothing to show that they were widely used. The favourite instruments of the Korean upper class, the *kŏmun'go, kayagŭm, taegŭm* and *pip'a,* were made of more perishable materials. Nevertheless, some traces might be expected to have been identified, even of objects made principally of wood and bamboo, for most of them unquestionably contained more durable metal parts. Yet among the royal tombs of the Three Kingdoms and Silla periods so far excavated scarcely any remnants of musical interest have been discovered.

Thirteen silver pieces found in the tomb of King Munyong (501–523 A.D.) near Kongju are described in the archaeological report on the excavation as the decorative covers for the top and bottom ends and the side edges of a set of zithers (fig. 10).[20] No traces were found of the wooden body or silk strings of any instrument but the authors propose, on the basis of the dimensions of the pieces, that the instruments were 1·2 metres in length and 18-20 cms in width. They would thus have been

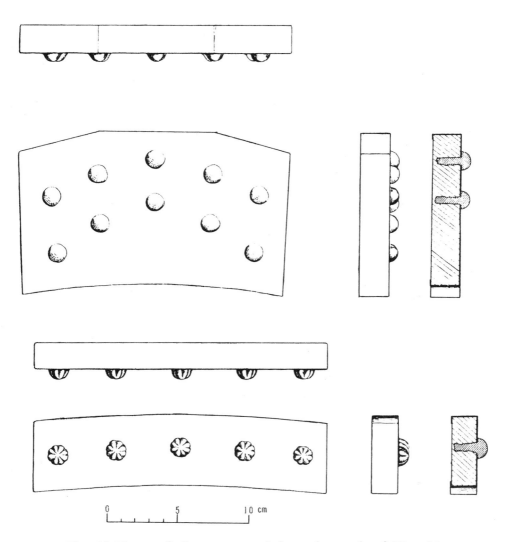

Fig. 10 Pieces of silver recovered from the tomb of King Munyong

similar in proportion to the *kŏmun'go* described in the *Akhak kwebŏm,* and perhaps to the Chinese *zheng*. Silver-plated, round-headed nails were driven home through each piece, ten in pairs at the top end and five at the bottom, apparently to fix the metal plates to the wooden body. Ten might seem an unnecessarily large number for fixing purposes alone, so that another functional or decorative purpose for the nails may be postulated. Judging by their size, shape and position flush with the surface of the metal they cannot be tuning pegs, yet their position does appear to suggest a five-stringed instrument. However, no five- or even ten-stringed instrument was in use in China at this time. The *guqin* already had seven strings and was of quite a different shape to that indicated by the silver pieces. Both the *zheng* and its relative the *zhu,* which had had five strings in the early Han dynasty, had twelve or thirteen in the 6th century (Hiyashi K. *(1)* p.169). The tomb contained two of the larger end-pieces and no less than eight of the smaller. It is hard to believe that the Paekche court would have preserved two examples of outdated Chinese instruments, let alone eight. According to the *Sui shu* both Paekche and Koguryŏ used the *zheng.* For Koguryŏ two versions are recorded, *danzheng* and *juzheng,* neither of which is described by literary sources so that their main features cannot be positively identified. The names may refer to the six- and four-stringed zithers discussed on page 224 below. If, however, it is accepted that one of these zithers is indicated by the name *wo konghou* and the other by one of the *zheng* names, then the second *zheng* name must still be accounted for. Is it perhaps possible that it refers to a surviving version of the old Chinese *zhu,* preserved in Korea because of its similarity to the *kŏmun'go* in terms of shape, approximate number of strings, and the fact that both were played with a short stick? The existence of a five-stringed zither in 5th-century Koguryŏ is supported by the picture of·the girl accompanying the singer in plate 109. It is tempting to make a tentative connection between this instrument and the silver pieces from King Munyong's tomb. However, only further archaeological evidence may finally determine whether these pieces do or do not have any musical relevance.

The National Museum, Tokyo and the Shōsōin Treasury at Nara preserve a small number of early Korean instruments, whilst jade flutes at the National Museum, Kyŏngju have been attributed to the Silla period. Some doubt about their actual age is

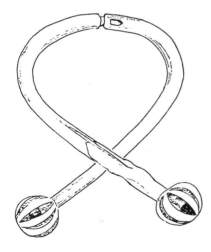

Fig. 11 Harness jingle or ritual object. 3rd century B.C.

Fig. 12 Eight - armed shaman bell. c. 3rd century B.C.

now admitted. Jade flutes in the National Museum, Kongju and the National Kyŏng-bok University Museum, Taegu are firmly attributed to the Chosŏn dynasty. A number of temple bells survive undamaged from the Silla and Koryŏ periods, but these were not instruments for musical performance any more than the harness jingles or shaman bells of which there are numerous early examples (figs. 11,12).

Three of the oldest authenticated instruments in Korea are the two pottery drums of the Koryŏ dynasty belonging to the National Museum and a 16th century *punch'ŏng* example in the Pusan City Museum.*

Akhak kwebŏm provides a detailed description of 57 instruments known in the 15th century, thirty seven under the heading of *aak*, thirteen under *tangak* and seven only under *hyangak*. This allocation must be based on the supposed origination of the instruments as much as on their function: By the end of the 15th century, for example, such popular instruments as the *ajaeng* and the *t'aep'yŏngso*, listed under *tangak*, were already being used in *hyangak*, and *hyangak* suites introduced at the Royal Ancestral Shrine in 1463 were enriched by the ringing tones of the bells and chimes of *aak*. A number of instruments are not mentioned in *Akhak kwebŏm* and may have developed after its publication.

Sixty instruments are currently preserved at the National Classical Music Institute, the majority of which are no longer in use. Space prevents a description of them all here, and the reader is advised to consult Chang *(1)*. On the following pages are shown some of the most important and interesting examples which are most likely to be heard in the performance of Korean music today. They are arranged in the traditional Sino-Korean order of the 'eight sounds' *(p'arum)*, the distinctive timbres resulting from the use of particular materials in their manufacture. Line drawings are taken from the first edition of *Akhak kwebŏm*, and show how little change has taken place in the style of the instruments over the last five hundred years.

* The Central Historical Museum at P'yŏngyang possesses a bone flute attributed to the bronze age, discovered at Kalpori in Northern Hamgyŏng Province. It is damaged at one end, but appears to have nine holes on its upper surface and a notch at the blowing end. (DPR Korean Cultural Properties Preservation Bureau, *Chaoxian zhongyang lishi bowuguan,* P'yŏngyang 1979, p.17)

4. Catalogue

A. METAL

1) P'yŏnjong

Sixteen bronze bells hang in two ranks of eight from a decorated wooden frame approximately 150 cms tall and 190 cms in length. The bells are eliptical in cross-section and all of the same size, differences in thickness determining their pitch, which rises in semi-tones from C(bottom right) to e^b(top left). The player, seated on the ground, strikes the bottom rim of a bell with a hammer made of horn at the point indicated by a circle. Though originally reserved for use at the Confucian ritual the bells also came to be used in other court ceremonies during the Chosŏn dynasty. Today they are still played at the Confucian Shrine and the Royal Ancestral Shrine and may also be heard in performances of *Pohŏja*, *Nagyangch'un* and *Yŏmillak*. A single, larger bell hanging from a frame, *t'ŭkchong*, is used together with the tub (*ch'uk*) and the *chin'go* drum as a starting signal to the orchestra on the terrace.

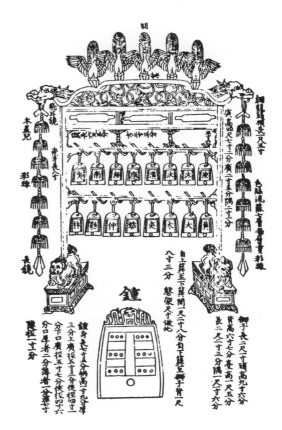

2) Panghyang

Consisting of sixteen iron slabs mounted in two ranks on a decorated wooden frame c.170 cms in height, this instrument announced the tune of *tangak* pieces before the

bells and chimes of *aak* were also adopted for this purpose, and continued to be used until the 20th century. Today it may only be heard at the Royal Ancestral Shrine. The slabs are fastened at one end by a loop to a metal cross-bar, and rest unfastened across a second cross-bar at the other end. They are struck with a hammer. Tuning is determined by thickness of the slabs:According to Chang (1) the range is from C to e^b, i.e. identical with that of the bells and chimes. Lee H.K. (2) p.50 gives the following variant pitches for the instruments used before and after the Hideyoshi invasions:

(i) Pre-invasion (from the first edition of *Akhak kwebŏm*)

9	10	11	12	13	14	15	16
B	c	d	e	f	c#	g#	d#

8	7	6	5	4	3	2	1
A#	A	G	F#	F	E	D	C

(ii) Post-invasion (from the 1620 edition of *Akhak kwebŏm*)

9	10	11	12	13	14	15	16
G#	c	d	e	d#	c#	f	g

8	7	6	5	4	3	2	1
A#	A	G	F#	F	D#	D	C

B. STONE

3) P'yŏn'gyŏng

The stone chimes are among the most ancient instruments in the Orient, dating back to the Chinese Shang and Zhou dynasties. Like the *p'yŏnjong* they were initially used in Korea for *aak* and later for *tangak* as well. Sixteen stones hang in two ranks of eight on a decorated wooden frame, c.150 cms tall and 190 cms long. The pair of ducks supporting the pedestals indicate that the chimes are 'civil' instruments and *yin* as opposed to the 'military', *yang* bells whose frame is supported by lions. The stones are suspended by a cord threaded through a hole near the point of the angle, so that their longer sides hang lower. The player, seated on the ground, faces the lower end of the stones, which he strikes with a horn hammer. The pitches of the stones, arranged to play in unison with the bells, may be altered by varying the length of the longer side in proportion to that of the shorter side. A single stone chime, *t'ŭkkyŏng,* stands on the

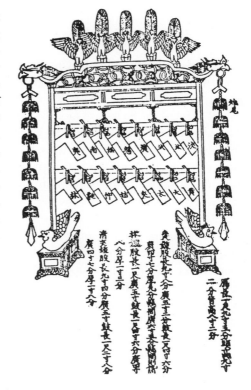

west side of the terrace at the Confucian Shrine and replaces the *t'ukchong* in the concluding percussion phrases of the music. It is larger than the regular stone chimes.

C. SILK

4) *Kŏmun'go*

This, possibly the oldest of native Korean instruments, is also the most respected, its player often being the most senior member of the orchestra. It is a wooden half tube zither approximately 150 cms in length and slightly tapering in width, with six strings of twisted silk and varying thickness. The second, third and fourth strings are stretched across sixteen fixed bridges and are tuned by circular pegs underneath the bottom end of the instrument. The remaining three are tuned by adjusting single, moveable bridges shaped like the clawed foot of a bird. The strings are plucked or struck with a short wooden plectrum, *sultae,* against a leather band covering the top end of the sounding board. The two strings that are the most important for playing the melody, numbers two and three, are pushed horizontally with

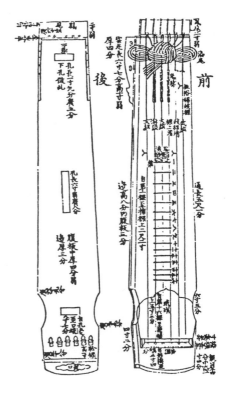

70

the fourth and middle fingers of the left hand to produce vibrato and slur. There are separate tuning systems for court and folk music, and the range of the *kŏmun'go* is from B^b to b$^{b''}$

5) *Kayagŭm*

The *kayagŭm* is regarded as the feminine, *yin* instrument complementing the masculine, *yang, kŏmun'go.* In traditional times scholars often preferred to play the latter, ladies the *kayagŭm,* but this distinction no longer applies. It is a half tube zither and exists in two forms, a larger one (c.160 cms long, 30 cms wide) for court music and a smaller, lighter one (c.142 cms long, 23 cms wide) for folk music and *sanjo.* The court instrument is distinguished by the 'ram's horns' at its bottom end, the steeper curvature of its top surface, and by the fact that it is made from a single piece of wood hollowed out. The wood is paulownia, used also for making the *ajaeng* and *kŏmun'go.* Both

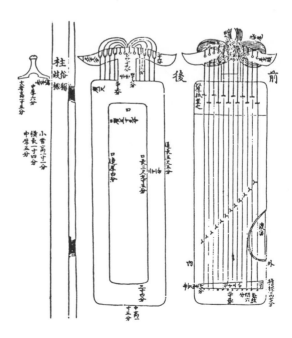

the *kŏmun'go* and the folk *kayagŭm,* however, have a bottom board of chestnut. The tone of the *kayagŭm* is lighter than that of the *kŏmun'go* and its compass (E^b-b^b') more limited. Its twelve strings of twisted silk are all stretched over moveable bridges and tied at the bottom end in an elaborate knot. They are tuned differently for court and folk music and are plucked with the fingers of the right hand, while the left hand twists and depresses them vertically to the left of the bridges to create a wide range of effects and to adjust the tuning. This may be done even in mid-performance. Lee Chae-suk, in her pioneering transcriptions of *kayagŭm sanjo,* devises symbols for fourteen uses of the left hand (Musical Example 7).

6) Ajaeng

Unlike its Chinese companion the *zheng,* the *ajaeng* came to play Korean as well as Chinese music and thus found a permanent place for itself in the Korean instrumentarium. It plays both court and folk music. The *ajaeng* is a wooden zither approximately 160 cms long, with seven strings of twisted silk stretched across moveable bridges and tuned from A^b-b^b. Unlike the *kŏmun'go* and the *kayagŭm* it does not rest on the

Musical Example 7. The opening bars of the Kim Chuk-p'a *kayagŭm sanjo*

player's knees but is supported at the right hand end by a wooden stand, and unlike the other two zithers its strings are not plucked but bowed with a resined stick of forsythia wood approximately 65 cms in length. The left hand is used to depress the strings, which varies the pitch and creates vibrato. The *ajaeng* has a rasping sound not dissimilar to that of the *haegŭm,* from which its name 'rasping zither' is derived: It is something of an acquired taste.

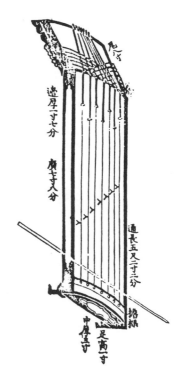

7) *Haegŭm*

The two-stringed fiddle of central Asian origin was in use in Korea by the 13th century and quickly established itself as a favourite instrument in both court and popular ensembles. It is approximately 70 cms in length from the top of its curved neck to the bottom of its soundbox. This may be made of hollowed out bamboo or of hardwood and is open at the rear. Two strings of twisted silk are stretched across the soundbox and tuned a fifth apart (A^b, e^b) by means of large wooden pegs. Older illustrations show these pegs positioned half way up the neck, compared with their modern position which is near the top. There is no fingerboard, the strings being pulled with the fingers of the left hand. The bow, of loosely woven horse hair, is threaded between the two strings. The player holds the *haegŭm* vertically, resting the soundbox on his left knee, and bows the strings horizontally.[21] It produces a rather harsh sound but is nevertheless capable of expressive tone, and is one of the most indispensable of instruments in almost any ensemble.

8) *Yanggŭm*

The dulcimer was introduced to China in the late Ming dynasty by Jesuit missionaries and reached Korea in the 18th century, when it was incorporated into ensembles for *Yŏngsan hoesang* and the refined lyric songs. It is the only instrument of the Korean orchestra to have metal strings, so that its inclusion in the 'silk' category may be unexpected. It is also the only instrument whose strings are hammered. There are fourteen quadruple strings, stretched alternately across one or other of the two fixed metal bridges. They are struck with a hammer of a flexible bamboo strip tipped with felt. Unlike the Chinese *yangqin,* the *yanggŭm* is not used as a virtuoso instrument and usually plays the tune without elaboration, doubling up with the *kayagŭm.*

D. BAMBOO

9) Taegŭm

The largest of the native Korean transverse flute family, the *taegŭm* is used in both court and folk music ensembles. Its *sanjo* is particularly popular. It measures approximately 80 cms and has six finger holes, a blowing hole and an additional hole covered with a membrane, which produces a distinctively 'breathy' sound. Heavy tremolo effects are produced by moving the head and the instrument itself, rather than by the manipulation of the cheeks and lips as in the case of the *p'iri*. Its range is B♭-e♭", the middle register and four notes of the upper register being played by overblowing. The *sogŭm* and the *tangjŏk* (the Chinese *di* flute, which plays in *tangak* and *Yŏngsan hoesang* and may have been the model for the original Silla flutes) are similar. They play an octave higher than the *taegŭm* and lack the membrane hole. The Japanese equivalent, though smaller, is the *kagurabue*.

10) Tanso

This short (c.40 cms) vertical flute is popular in chamber ensembles and in a duet with the *saenghwang* and a trio with the *yanggŭm* and *haegŭm*. It has a notched lip and five finger holes, the first of which is on the reverse. It has a soft, delicate tone and in performance its range extends from a$^{b'}$-a$^{b'''}$. It is not illustrated in *Akhak kwebŏm* and may date from the 19th century.

11) Hyangp'iri

Three double reed oboes are known in Korea. *Hyangp'iri* ('native oboe') is the largest of them (c.27 cms long), and because of its powerful and expressive dynamic range it often leads orchestral ensembles in the announcement of the tune. Its tone may be

warm and mellow or strident and piercing, and a strong vibrato is obtained by movement of the lips and control of the air in the cheeks. Its long (c.7 cms) double reed is bound by a copper band and inserted into the upper end of the bamboo pipe at a slight downward angle. The pipe has eight finger holes, the first of which is on the reverse. Its compass is limited, A^b-f'. Its relative the *sep'iri* is a more slender instrument producing a softer tone, and the *tangp'iri* ('Chinese oboe') a shorter, fatter version with a range of C-a' used in *tangak* pieces. Despite their names all three instruments probably originated in central Asia and the first of them arrived in Korea during the Koguryŏ period. Its Japanese counterpart is the *hichiriki*.

12) *So* 'panpipes'

This instrument, so well known in many parts of the world, made its first appearance from China as far back as the Koguryŏ period and was again included in the gifts of 1114 and 1116, yet it never seems to have achieved widespread currency in Korea and is limited nowadays to use at the Confucian Shrine. In its extant form the sixteen notched bamboo pipes are arranged symetrically with the shortest in the middle and the longest at the outer sides, the wooden casing still closely resembling that shown in the *Akhak kwebŏm*. It plays C-d$^\#$, the same range as the bells and chimes.

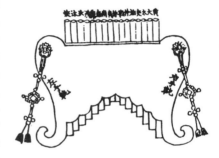

E. GOURD

13) *Saenghwang*

The mouthorgan, common in this form to China, Korea and Japan and related to the much larger mouthorgans of south east Asia, consists of a windchest once made of a gourd but now of wood or metal. Seventeen bamboo pipes of varying length are inserted vertically into the top of the windchest and a short mouthpiece into the side. One of the pipes is mute, the remainder sounding one note each to complete a compass of $e^{b'}$-c'''. A note is produced by stopping the hole at the base of a tube, so that air is directed across a metal tongue which vibrates inside the tube. It may be sounded by inhaling as well as exhaling and is the only east Asian instrument that can play clusters of notes, though in Korea it does not do so. It is difficult to play, less popular than it used to be, and is now confined mostly to performances of ritual music and a chamber duet with the *tanso*.

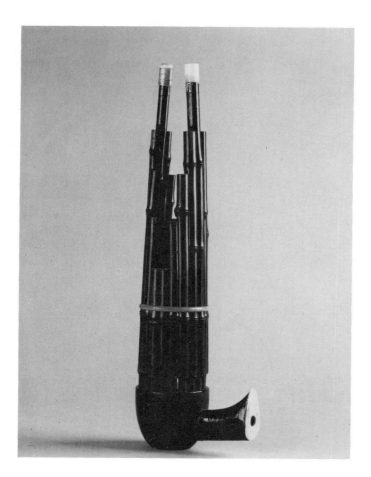

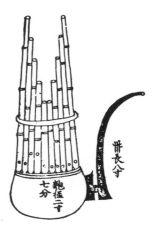

F. POTTERY

14) Hun

The earliest literary evidence for the existence of the ocarina in Korea refers to its inclusion in Emperor Huizong's gift of 1114. However, it had been known in China since before the Shang dynasty, and confirmation that this simple instrument had spread to the peninsula at some early point is provided by a finely made, decorated example from Korea preserved at the National Museum, Tokyo (fig.13). The *hun* is a globular flute of baked clay, with a blowing hole on top, two finger holes in the rear and three in the front. It is held in the cupped hands and has an effective range of one octave. It produces a rather mournful tone, and nowadays its use is restricted mainly to the Confucian ceremonies, where it doubles up with the small flute with a mouthpiece, *chi*.

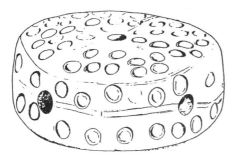

Fig. 13 Globular flute,
7th – 9th century A.D.

G. WOOD

15) T'aep'yŏngso

This double-reed oboe with a conical, metal bell and a wooden pipe is closely related to the Chinese *suona* and similar instruments in India and the Middle East. It may have reached China during the Mongol period (13th-14th century), and has enjoyed wide popularity at all kinds of outdoor events, from military and farmers' music to ancestral shrine music. It has seven fingerholes on the front and one on the rear, and like the *p'iri* it has a restricted range of A^b-e$^{b'}$. Unlike the *p'iri* its reed is short and narrow. It has a strident tone not unlike that of the *p'iri*, but it lacks the subtlety of which the latter is capable, and is usually confined to outdoor occasions. It is approximately 47 cms long.

16) Pak 'clappers'

The purpose of this percussion instrument, handled by the 'conductor' of the traditional orchestra, is to start and stop the music and to indicate the beginning of a new movement or rhythmic pattern, as in *Yŏngsan hoesang*. The 'conductor''s only function during a performance is to play the *pak*. Its six wooden slats (c. 40 cms by 7 cms) are bound loosely together at their thinner end by a leather thong of deerskin. They are held vertically, bound end uppermost, and spread apart before being clapped together with a sharp movement of the elbows and wrists, once to start a piece of music and three times to end it.

17) Ch'uk   *18) Ŏ*

The *ch'uk*, 'tub', like the *ŏ* 'tiger' (no.18), is one of the most ancient Chinese percussion instruments, dating perhaps from the Shang dynasty. It consists of a wooden box, the sides of the top surface being longer (55 cms) than those of the bottom (43 cms), raised off the ground on a stand to a height of approx. 80 cms. A circular pole protrudes through a hole in the middle of the top surface and is lifted and lowered by the player to thump the base of the tub. It is used at the Confucian and Ancestral Shrine ceremonies, where three beats mark the beginning of a musical passage.

The *ŏ* is shaped like a tiger crouched on a base. Nowadays it is made of wood, but in the past it was sometimes made of clay. It is approx. 100 cms long and 40 cms high. Along its backbone is a line of 27 serrations. The player strikes the tiger's head three times with a split bamboo brush and then scrapes it along the back from neck to tail, to bring to an end passages of music at the Confucian and Ancestral Shrines.

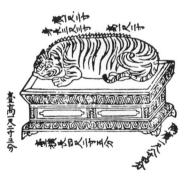

INTRODUCTION

H. SKIN

19) Chin'go

Since the loss of the last *kŏn'go* (see note to plate 32) during the Korean War, this has been the largest of the Korean drums, having a diameter of c. 110 cms. It has a head of cowskin, which is beaten with a large, cloth-covered hammer. Its use is confined to the courtyard orchestra at the Confucian ceremonies where, together with the *pak*, the *nodo* drum and the *ch'uk* tub it begins the musical performance, marks every fourth beat as punctuation, and with the *pak, nodo* and *ŏ* tiger ends it. The *nodo* consists of two barrel drums transfixed at right angles to each other by a pole, each having two leather cords fastened to the sides of the body. When the pole is twirled, the cords beat against the drumheads.

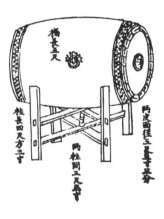

20) Chwago

Medium-sized Korean barrel drums may be suspended either horizontally on a four-legged frame (like the *kyobanggo* used for the drum dance and seen in plate 5) or vertically on a square frame. The *chwago* is the most common example of the latter. It first appears in an 18th century picture by Kim Hong-do and is now frequently used

84

in orchestral ensembles to reinforce the beat of the *changgo*. It normally stands, sideways on, at the left of the orchestra. The player sits to the right of it and beats it with a soft-headed stick held in his right hand. 19th century *ŭigwe* illustrations of this drum, such as the one seen below, call it the *kyobanggo*. The 15th century *Akhak kwebŏm*, however, whilst making no mention of a *chwago*, uses the term *kyobanggo* as it is used today to describe a horizontal frame drum (bottom, left). *Ŭigwe* sources simply call this a *mugo* 'dance drum' (bottom, right).

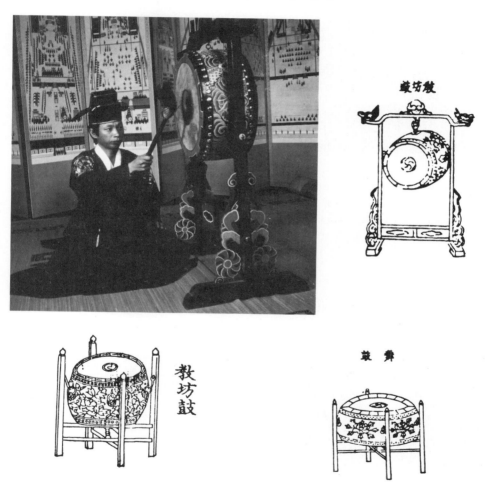

21) *Puk* (or *yonggo* 'dragon drum')

This is a small double-headed barrel drum used in rural bands and for the accompaniment of *p'ansori*. Its heads are covered in cowskin and measure 34-40 cms in diameter. It is 20-25 cms deep. Like the *changgo* it may be hung across the shoulder for

use in processions and dances, or stood on its side when the player is seated. The *p'ansori* accompanist beats the left head with the palm of his hand and the right head, and its wooden rim, with a stick.

22) *Changgo* 'stick drum'

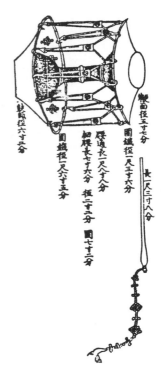

The hourglass drum has been one of the most familiar sights in pictures of east Asian music for nearly one and a half millenia. In Korea it exists at present in two standard versions, the heavier one for orchestral use, the lighter as a portable instrument for use in *nongak*. Larger drums may measure over 60 cms in length and have a diameter of over 30 cms, smaller ones approximately one third less. The *changgo* is usually painted red, although some instruments used in *nongak* are left unpainted to display the natural wood. The orchestral drum stands on the floor, the player sitting behind it. The left head, usually of cowskin, is thicker than the right and produces a dull sound when struck with the palm of the hand. The right head, or its rim, is beaten or rolled with a thin stick and gives a sharper, more distinct note. It may be made of sheep or dogskin. The tension of this head is adjusted by moving the leather girdles that grip the strings. The portable drum is carried on the player's left hip by a strap hung across the right shoulder. Its heads are tuned to equal tension. The one on the left is struck with a round-headed mallet, the one on the right with a stick, although the player will sometimes cross hands and use his mallet to beat the right head.

Notes to pp. 1~87

1. The dates on which the three kingdoms are said to have officially accepted Buddhism are Koguryŏ 372 A.D., Paekche 384, Silla 527. On cultural links with a Buddhist flavour between the southern China coast and Paekche see A.L. Julians, *Teng-Hsien: an important Six Dynasties tomb,* Artibus Asiae 1980 pp.30-32.

2. According to *SS* (15, p.380) the Koguryŏ band at Chang'an consisted of the *tanjaeng* (Ch. *danzheng*) zither, *sugonghu* (Ch. *shu konghou*) vertical harp, *wagonhu* (Ch. *wo konghou*) horizontal harp, *pip'a* (Ch. *pipa*) lute, *ohyŏn* (Ch. *wuxian*) lute (or zither: See p.241), *chŏk* (Ch. *di*) flute, *saeng* (Ch. *sheng*) mouthorgan, *so* (Ch. *xiao*) panpipes, *sop'iri*(Ch. *xiao bili*) small oboe (later known in Korea as the *tangp'iri*), *top'i p'iri (Ch. taopi bili)* 'peachskin oboe' (later known in Korea as the *hyangp'iri*), *yogo* (Ch. *yaogu*) waistdrum, *chego* (Ch. *qigu*) drum, *t'ango* (Ch. *dangu*) portable pole-drum, and the *p'ae* (Ch. *bei*) shell. *SGSG* (32.11b-12a), quoting *Tong dian,* adds a 'double-handed' zither *kukchaeng* (Ch. *juzheng*), a *taep'iri* (Ch. *da bili*) 'big oboe', and a flute with an artificial mouthpiece *uich'wijŏk* (Ch. *izui di*).

   Paekche instruments comprised the *kak* (Ch. *jue*) horn, a harp, a zither, the large mouthorgan *u* (Ch. *yu*), the *chŏk* flute, *chi* (Ch. *chi*) flute, and an oboe (*SS* 81 p.1818; *SGSG* 32.12b).

3. *BS* 82 p.3118

4. *SS* 15 p.377

5. *SGSG* 32.5b This passage devotes considerable attention to the music of Silla, which had had a long history before unification. It is first mentioned in connection with celebrations occurring in 28 A.D. (*SGSG* 1.6b-7a).

6. A further piece of evidence about the music of Silla before unification is a little more ambiguous. It also comes from *SGSG :*
   > Little is known about Master Paekkyŏl [a Silla musician during the reign of King Chabi (458-478)]. He lived at the foot of Mount Nang and was very poor. Since he wore patched and tattered clothes, like suspended quails, the people in the eastern village called him Paekkyŏl Sŏnsaeng, or Master with a Hundred Patch Clothes. He admired the character of Yong Qiji [a Chinese *guqin* player] and enjoyed himself with a zither. He expressed his joy, sorrow, anger and complaint by playing the zither. It was

the end of the year, when neighbours pounded millet into flour. Listening to the sound of the pestle, his wife said : "Everyone has grain to pound but we have nothing. How can we see the old year out?" Looking up to heaven the Master sighed and said : "Death and life are ordained. Riches and honour depend upon heaven. We cannot reject their coming, nor can we pursue their going. Why are you distressed? I will make the sound of the pestle so as to console you." Thereupon he took his zither and produced the sound of a pestle. The composition spread and was called *Taeak*, or 'Pestle Music' (48.3b-4a).

The charitable conclusion from this story would be that it shows the versatility of the composer. On the other hand, if *Taeak* were a well known example of Silla music, it is not hard to believe that it might remind critics in the rival states of the primitive and maligned music once practised in the notorious Chinese state of Qin (3rd century B.C.): "The beating of earthen jugs, knocking on jars, plucking of the *zheng*, and striking on thigh bones, the while singing 'Wu! Wu!' as a means of delighting the ear and eye, such indeed was the music of Qin" (*Shi ji* 87, pp.2543-4).

7. Part of the inscription cast on the enormous bronze bell for Pongdŏksa in 771 A.D., which records the exemplary rule of King Sŏngdŏk, says that "proper ceremonies and music accompanied all his ways." The earliest specific reference to the study of Chinese music by Koreans dates from 664 (*Samguksa chŏryo*, Asea Munhwasa, Seoul, 1973, p.10.6a). It is reasonable to assume that in the 8th century 'proper ceremonies and music' were both Korean and Chinese. The bell, the largest in Korea, is better known as the Emille Bell and hangs at the National Museum, Kyŏngju. It is 3.75 metres high and weighs 20 tons.

8. ed. Ji Liankang, *Yue ji*, Renmin Yinyue Chubanshi, Beijing 1982, pp.9, 34, 39

9. More than one hundred pieces of 15th century Korean music have been preserved in King Sejo's notational system. They have all been transcribed for modern western performance in Condit (3).

10. There is no thorough treatment of Korean dance in any western language although Heyman (1) is handy. In the 15th century moralists were intent on cleaning up the performance of dance as well as the texts of music. James Scarth Gale quotes Nam Hyo-on's reaction to the current tendency towards what he saw as over-relaxation in court dance :

> We Koreans have learned the dances of the barbarians in which we bob our heads and roll our eyes, hump our backs and work our bodies, legs, arms and fingertips. We shut them up and shoot them out, bound after bound, like a twanging bow. Then, bouncing forth like dogs, we run. Bearlike, we stand upright, and then, like birds with outstretched wings, we swoop.
>
> From highest lords of state down to the lowest music-girl all have learned these dances and take delight therein. They are called *homu*, the Wild Man's Dances, and are accompanied by instruments of music. At first I rather favoured them myself, though my dead friend, An Cha-jong, was much opposed. Said he, "Man's attempt thus to

show himself off is unworthy of a human being. Such actions lower him to the level of the beast. Why should I take my body and put it through the motions of an animal?'' I thought this remark somewhat extreme until I read, in the *Han Shu*, Ho Tz'u-kung's comment on seeing Lord Tan Ch'ang perform the dance called 'Monkey's Bath' (Richard Rutt, *James Scarth Gale and his History of the Korean People*, Royal Asiatic Society, Seoul, 1972, p.240.).

11. *Sangyŏngsan, Chungyŏngsan* and *Seryŏngsan* are three movements from *Yŏngsan hoesang.*

12. Even the Scottish missionary James Scarth Gale hints at the same sort of feeling:

One of the noticeable features of Korean life is the dancing-girl. You see her in the street dressed in all her fluff and feathers, coloured like a bird in green and pink and yellow. She appears thus in all the colours of the rainbow, tipped with ermine edges: a picture for the eye to see, not often pretty in feature from the western point of view, but striking... She is as blithe a bird as ever hopped, with never a shadow across her easy-sitting conscience; happy in the role she is called upon to play, and feeling that she is a very important part of what the east calls 'society'. If we reckon her cultural ancestry according to the books and documents on hand, she is a thousand years old; and as far as physical ancestry is concerned, she probably comes down from some of the best families of the day in which her fathers lived (Rutt, *ibid.*, p.277).

13. In the late 15th century the Royal Music Institute (*Changagwŏn*) had employed 971 musicians. By the mid-17th century the number had fallen to 619 (Song B.S.*(1)*).

14. Four additional pieces, three of them based on the orchestral composition *Pohŏja*, may be played in place of the regular first four. This version, less common than the other three, is known as *Pyŏlgok*, 'Alternative tunes'.

15. Lee Hye-Ku's most important research writings on *Yŏngsan hoesang* are to be found in two articles republished in *EKTM*, '*Yŏngsan hoesang*: a Comparison of the Modern Piece and the Version Notated in the *Taeak hubo* (1759)' and '*Chung Yŏngsan* as a Variation of *Sang Yŏngsan*', and in the booklet (56pp.) accompanying a four-record set of all three versions and *Pyŏlgok*, played by Chŏngnong Akhoe and issued by SEM Gramophone, Seoul, 1982 (SEL 100 122).

16. Notes accompanying 'Korean Buddhist Music', Vogue record LVLX-253, 1964

17. *P'algwanhoe* was an important national rite during which shamans prayed for the peace of the country. See *KRS* 69.12a ff. In 1073 the Chinese ball-throwing game *paoqiu yue* was introduced into it. *KRS* 9.11a.

18. In contrast to court dance the masked dance dramas of Korea have been the subject of much attention by English-language writers. Articles include Lee D.H. (1) (2); Cho Oh-kon, 'A Mask-dance Theater of North-eastern Korea', *KJ* 21 no.12, 1981 pp.45-8; Cho Oh-kon, 'The

Mask-dance Theater from Hwanghae Province', *KJ* 22 no.5, 1982 pp.36-45.

19. The study of modes in traditional Korean music is fraught with difficulties, and so far the subject has neither been fully researched by Korean musicologists nor systematically summarised in any English-language publication. *Akhak kwebŏm* points out the theoretical possibility of sixty modes from a pentatonic scale recognising twelve pitches. *Samguk sagi* names two used for *kayagŭm* music, two for *kŏmun'go* and three for *pip'a*. In the 15th century seven were again in common use, though not exactly the same seven as those of the Silla period. Four of them, according to Yi Tŭg-yun (1620) were the most common, corresponding to the four seasons and "promoting all creation" (*SRKM* p.118). Their names were *p'yŏngjo, naksijo, kyemyŏnjo* and *ujo*. *P'yŏngjo* and *ujo* were the *kŏmun'go* modes referred to by *Samguk sagi*, but not only did the definition of modal structures change from period to period, so that Silla *ujo* was by no means the same as that of the early Chosŏn dynasty or again of the 20th century, but even the usage of certain terms extended beyond that of simple nomenclature to include what were presumably derived descriptive qualities. For example, in *Akhak kwebŏm naksijo* and *ujo* are both names of modes in their own right, as well as being modifiers of the modal term *p'yŏngjo* to indicate use of the mode in, respectively, a low register (keys of G, A^b, B^b and C) and a high register (keys of C, D, E^b and F). The two most common modes used in Korea today are a *do*-mode, *p'yŏngjo* (CDFGA) and a *re*-mode, *kyemyŏnjo* (CE^{b}FGB^b).
See Sur (1); Song B.S.(2) chapter 3; Lee H.K., 'Modes in early Korean Music Sources', *EKTM* pp.43-70; '*Ujo* in Modern *Kagok*', *ibid.* pp.71-84; '*Kyemyŏnjo* in Modern *Kagok*', *ibid.* pp.85-102.

20. Munhwajae Kwalliguk, *Munyongwang nung*, Seoul 1974, pp.41-2

21. An unusual front-view of court musicians in an early 19th century *ŭigwe* publication shows the *haegŭm* players all holding their instruments with the neck at an angle of 10° off the vertical, ⟨△⟩ . *HUCC* 3, *Chagyongjŏn chinjak chongnye ŭigwe*, Kungnip Kugagwŏn, Seoul, 1983 p.168.

SECTION TWO

The Plates

PLATE 1 The terrace orchestra at the Confucian Shrine

PLATE 2 Dancers at the Confucian Shrine

PLATE 3 The courtyard orchestra at the Royal Ancestral Shrine

PLATE 4
The sword dance

PLATE 5 The drum dance

PLATE 6 Seoul City Traditional Orchestra

PLATE 7 *Kayagŭm sanjo*

97

PLATE 8 *Kagok*

PLATE 9 *P'ansori*

PLATE 10 The Buddhist
cymbal dance

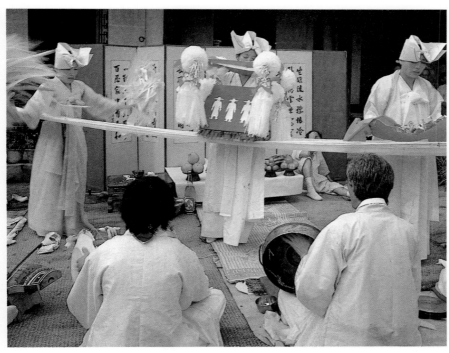

PLATE 11 A shaman *kut*

PLATE 12 Shaman dance, folk version

PLATE 13 *Nongak*

PLATE 14 Masked dance drama

PLATE 15 *Kodŏng* horns

PLATE 16 Silver pieces from the tomb of King Munyong

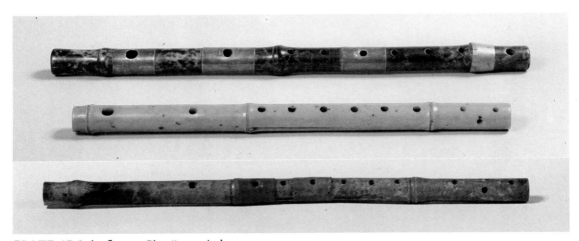

PLATE 17 Jade flutes, Chosŏn period

102

PLATE 18 *Punch'ŏng* pottery drum, Koryŏ period

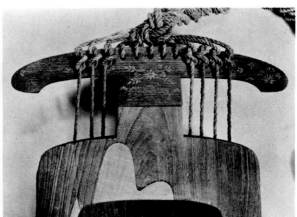

PLATE 19 *Kayagŭm*, Silla period

PLATE 20 The lord's procession. Anak. A.D.357

PLATE 21 Processional musicians.
Tŏkhŭngni. A.D.409

PLATE 22 Processional musicians.
Susanri. 5th century A.D.

PLATE 23 Princess Chonghyo's musicians. Helongxian. 9th century A.D.

PLATE 24 Court audience.
17th century

PLATE 25 Detail of plate 24

PLATE 26 Reception for ministers. 18th century

PLATE 27 Reception for ministers. 18th century

PLATE 28 Court banquet and entertainment. 18th century

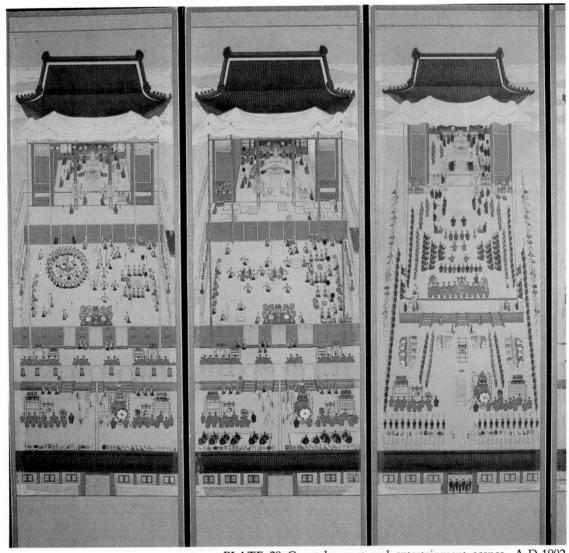

PLATE 29 Court banquet and entertainment scenes. A.D.1902

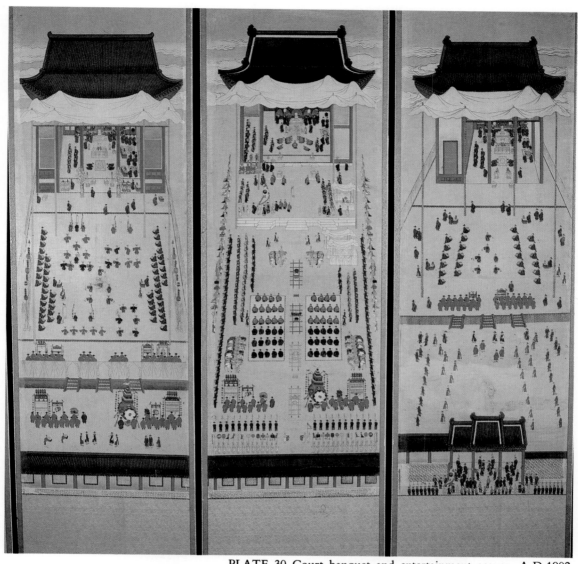

PLATE 30 Court banquet and entertainment scenes. A.D.1902

PLATE 31 Detail of plate 29

PLATE 32 Detail of plate 29

112

PLATE 33 Detail of plate 30

PLATE 34 Detail of plate 30

PLATE 35 Kim Hong-do, *Celebrations at the inauguration of the Governor of P'yŏngyang.*
18th-19th century

PLATE 36 Kim Hong-do,
*Party for the elderly at the foot of
Songaksan.* A.D.1804

PLATE 37 Detail of plate 36

PLATE 38 Banquet for officials. A.D.1533

PLATE 39 Entertainment at a meeting of the Society for the Elderly and Brave. A.D.1585

萬曆乙酉豆秋

117

PLATE 40 Banquet for the elderly. A.D.1623

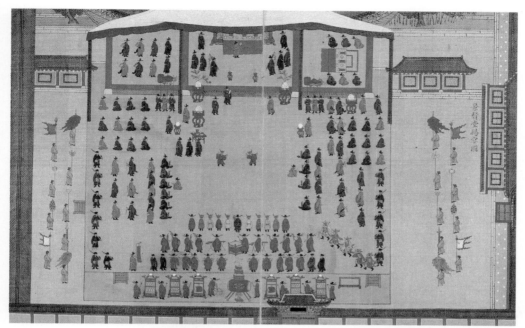

PLATE 41 Royal banquet for the Society of the Elderly. A.D.1730

PLATE 42 Detail of plate 41

PLATE 43 Meeting of the Society of the Elderly. A.D.1720

PLATE 44 Banquet given by the royal family. A.D.1744

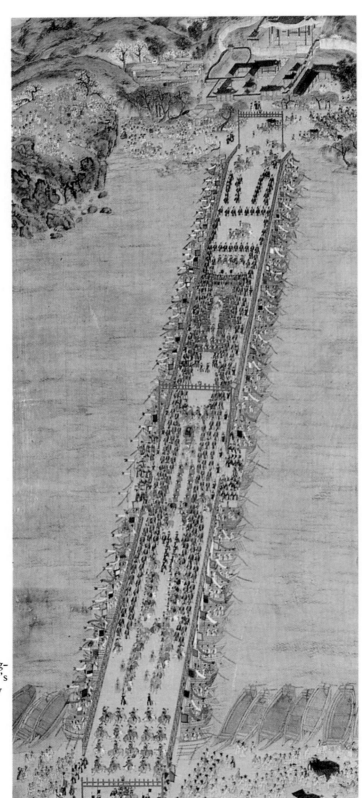

PLATE 45 King Chŏng-jo's visit to his father's tomb. 18th-19th century

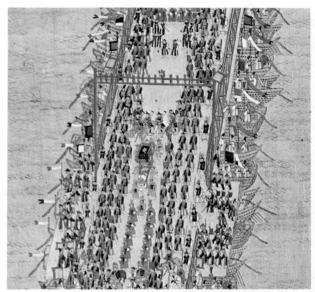

PLATE 46 Detail of plate 45

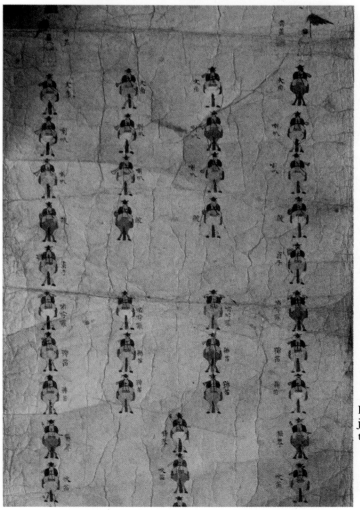

PLATE 47 King Chŏng-jo's visit to his father's tomb. A.D.1811

123

PLATE 49 Further detail of the above

PLATE 50 Further detail of the above

PLATE 48 attr. Ch'ŏng Son, *Greeting Japanese envoys at Dongnae* (detail). 18th century

PLATE 51 Korean envoy's procession to
Japan (detail). A.D.1636

PLATE 52 Further detail of the above

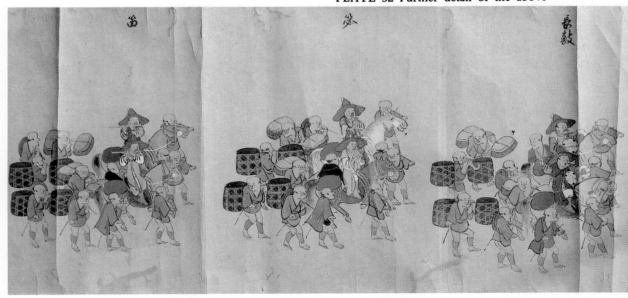

PLATE 53 After Kim Tuk-sin, *Playing music for Guo Fenyang*. Chosŏn dynasty

PLATE 54 attr. Kim Hong-do,
*Procession of the newly successful
graduate.* A.D.1781

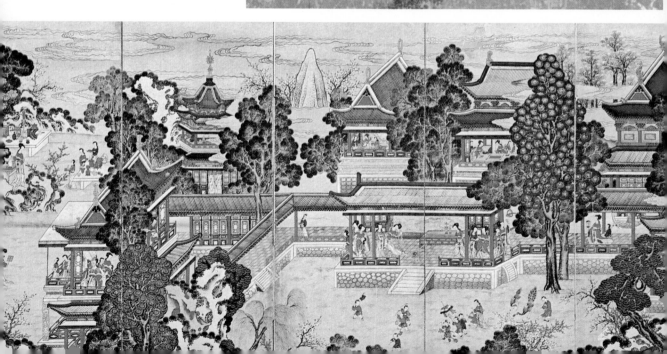

PLATE 55 Anon., *Procession of the newly successful graduate* (detail). 19th century

PLATE 56 Anon., *Procession of the newly appointed magistrate*. 19th century

PLATE 58 Detail of plate 57

PLATE 57 View of P'yŏngyang castle. 19th century

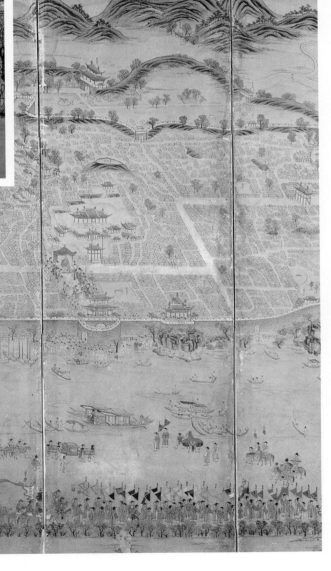

PLATE 59 Detail of plate 57

PLATE 60 Hunting scene. 19th century

131

PLATE 61 Anon., *Pak Yŏn and his wife*. Chosŏn dynasty

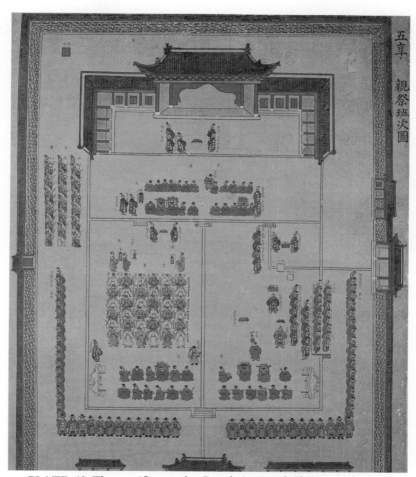

PLATE 62 The sacrifice at the Royal Ancestral Shrine. 19th century

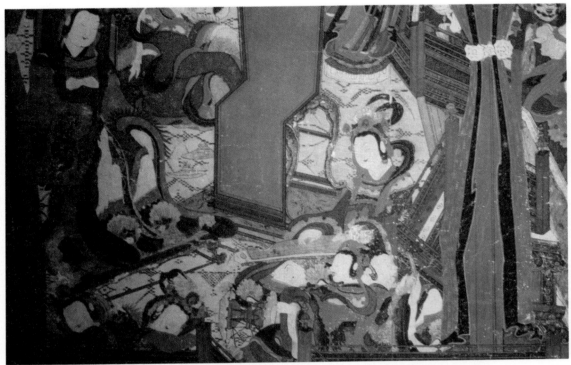

PLATE 63 Scene from the life of Buddha. 18th century

PLATE 64 Scenes from daily life : Buddhist
procession. 20th century

PLATE 65 Scenes from daily life : monks
chanting sutras. 20th century

PLATE 66 Scenes from daily life : monks' cymbal dance. A.D.1865

PLATE 67 Scenes from daily life : monks with large drum. 18th century

PLATE 68 Scenes from daily life : shaman and musicians. 18th century

PLATE 69 Scenes from daily life : shaman and musicians. 19th century

PLATE 70 Sin Yun-bok, *Shaman and musicians*. 18th-19th century

PLATE 71 Sin Yun-bok, *Buddhist beggar with large drum*. 18th-19th century

PLATE 72 Oxherd playing a flute. Early 20th century

PLATE 73 Deva playing a horn. 5th-6th century

PLATE 74-75 Deva musicians on a stone Amitabha Trinity. A.D.673

PLATE 76 Deva musicians. A : *saenghwang*
B : *chŏ* C : *pip'a* D : small cymbals. Silla
period

PLATE 77 Deva musician playing a *saenghwang*. 9th century A.D.

PLATE 78 Deva musicians. A : *pip'a*
B : *p'iri* A.D.904

A

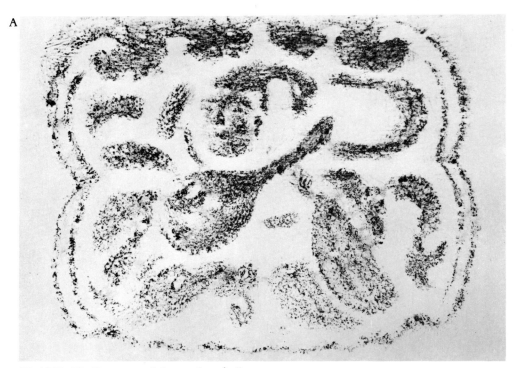

PLATE 79 Deva musicians. A : *ohyŏn
pip'a* B : *saenghwang* C : *konghu* D : *chŏ.*
Koryŏ period

B

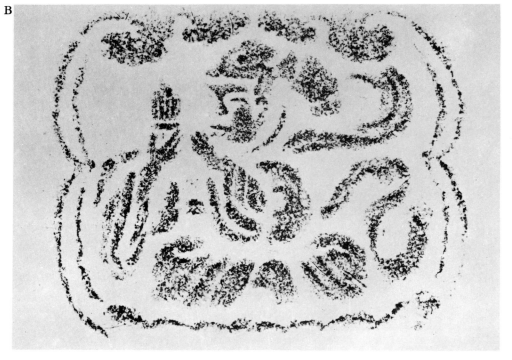

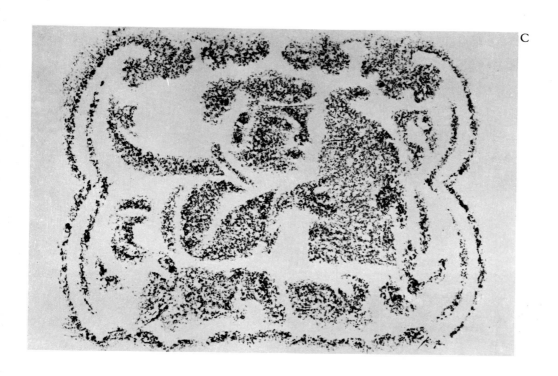

C

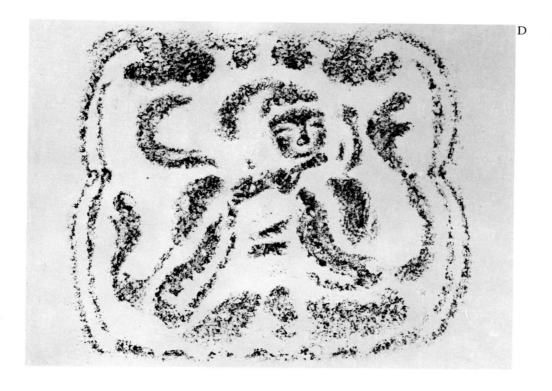

D

145

PLATE 81 Detail of plate 80 showing deva musicians playing a *konghu* and a *saenghwang*

PLATE 80 Bronze temple bell. A.D.725

146

PLATE 82 Deva musician playing a *pip'a*. 9th century A.D.

PLATE 83 Deva musician playing the small cymbals. 9th century A.D.

PLATE 84 Deva musicians playing a *saeng-hwang* and a flute. 9th century A.D.

PLATE 85 Deva flautist. 8th century A.D.

PLATE 86 Bronze sarira case. A.D.628

PLATE 87 Figures from the corners of the bronze sarira case (plate 86)' A : *yogo* B : small cymbals C : *chŏ* D : *pip'a*

PLATE 88 Deva flautist. Silla period

PLATE 89 Deva musician playing a *saenghwang*.
18th century

PLATE 90 Deva drummer.
18th century

PLATE 91 Deva drummer.
19th century

PLATE 92 Deva musician playing a *nabal*. 19th century

PLATE 93 Deva musician carrying a *haegŭm*. 20th century

PLATE 94 Deva musicians playing a *kayagŭm* and a vertical flute. 19th century

PLATE 95 Attendants on Amitabha Buddha in the Pure Land Paradise.
A.D.1323

156

PLATE 96 Attendants on Buddha. 18th century

PLATE 97 Guardian King holding a *pip'a*. 11th-12th century

PLATE 98 Guardian
King holding a *pip'a*.
18th century

PLATE 99 Guardian King holding
a *pip'a*. 20th century

PLATE 101 Kim Hong-do, *Immortals*. 18th-19th century

PLATE 102 Kim Hong-do, *Immortals*. 18th-19th century

PLATE 103 Kim Yang-gi, *Immortal playing a saenghwang*. Late 18th century

PLATE 104 The God of Longevity. Chosŏn dynasty

PLATE 106 Detail of plate 105.
A zither player

PLATE 105 Pottery jar decorated with figures. 5th-6th century

PLATE 107 Lid of a steamer decorated with figures. Silla period

PLATE 108 Horn player
Anak. A.D.357

PLATE 109 Lady with a servant carrying a zither.
Chang Chuan. Late 5th century A.D.

PLATE 110 Dancer. Anak. A.D.357

PLATE 111 Zither player and dancer. Chang Chuan. Late 5th century A.D.

PLATE 112 Dancers. Tonggou. 6th century A.D.

PLATE 113 Kim Chung-gun, *Kŏmun'go player*. 19th century

妓彈琴

PLATE 114 Sin Yun-bok, *Girl stringing a kŏmun'go*. 18th–19th century

PLATE 115 Sin Yun-bok,
Picnic by the lotus pond.
18th-19th century

PLATE 116 Sin Yun-bok,
Kisaeng with a saenghwang.
18th-19th century

PLATE 117 Sin Yun-bok,
Kisaeng by a lotus pond.
18th-19th century

PLATE 118 Anon., *Picnic in
the back garden.* 18th century

173

PLATE 119 Yi Kyŏng-yun, *Looking at the moon*. 16th century

PLATE 120 Yi Pang-un, *Playing the zither under a pine tree*. 18th-19th century

PLATE 121 Kim Hong - do, *Tanwŏn Pavilion*. 18th - 19th century

PLATE 122 Steamer with figure playing a lute. 5th-6th century A.D.

PLATE 123 Pottery lute player.
5th-6th century A.D.

PLATE 124 Yi Kyŏng-yun,
Playing the pip'a in a boat.
16th century

PLATE 125 Kim Hong-do, *Scholar playing the pip'a.* 18th-19th century

PLATE 126 Flute player.
5th-6th century A.D.

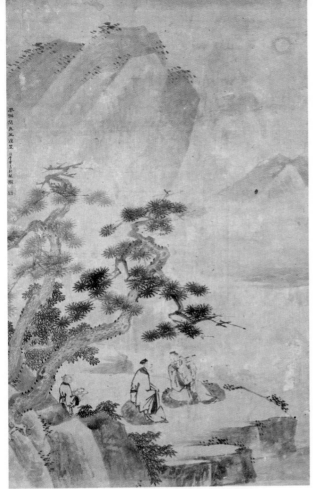

PLATE 127 Chin Che-hai, *Playing a flute in the moonlight*. 18th century

PLATE 128 Kim Ung-an, *Listening to a flute on the river bank*. 18th century

PLATE 129 Kim Hong-do, *Dancing boy*. 18th-19th century

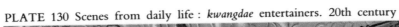

PLATE 130 Scenes from daily life : *kwangdae* entertainers. 20th century

PLATE 131 Scenes from daily life : tightrope walker. 18th century

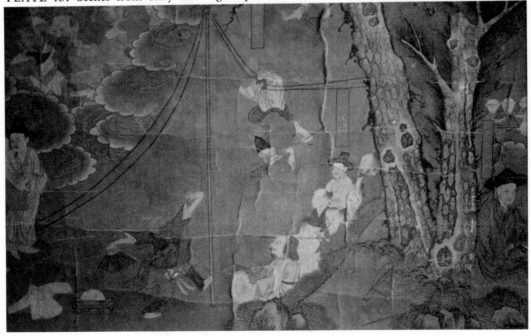

PLATE 132 Anon., *Masked dancers*. A.D.1724

PLATE 133 Anon., *P'ansori performance*. 19th century

塲唱客歌

PLATE 134 Kim Chung-gun, *P'ansori*. 19th century

184

PLATE 135 Sin Yun-bok, *Sword dance*. 18th-19th century

PLATE 136 Sin Yun-bok, *Music and dance*. 18th-19th century

PLATE 137 Sin Yun-bok, *Musical ensemble*. 18th-19th century

PLATE 138 attr. An
Kyŏn, *Landscape at Chipi*.
15th century

PLATE 139
Detail of plate 138

PLATE 140 Sin Yun-bok, *Boating scene*. 18th-19th century

PLATE 141-142 Kim
Sŏk-sin, *Music and dance
in mid-stream* (detail).
18th-19th century

Notes to the Plates

1. Music in Contemporary Performance

PLATE 1 The terrace orchestra at the Confucian Shrine *(Munmyoak)*

PLATE 2 Dancers at the Confucian Shrine *(Munmyoak)*

PLATE 3 The courtyard orchestra at the Royal Ancestral Shrine (*Chŏngmyoak*)

PLATE 4 The sword dance (*kŏmmu*). National Classical Music Institute, Seoul

PLATE 5 The drum dance (*mugo*). National Classical Music Institute, Seoul

PLATE 6 Performance of *Yŏngsan hoesang*. Seoul City Traditional Orchestra

PLATE 7 *Kayagŭm sanjo*. Senior student of the College of Music, Seoul National University

PLATE 8 *Kagok*. National Classical Music Institute, Seoul

PLATE 9 *P'ansori*

PLATE 10 The Buddhist cymbal dance

PLATE 11 A shaman with musicians performing at a *kut* on Cheju Island

PLATE 12 Folk dance version of a shaman dance

PLATE 13 *Nongak*

PLATE 14 Masked dance drama, *kosŏng ogwangdae*

PLATE 15 *Kodŏng,* an instrument used to accompany bull-head fighting in the folk-lore festival at Yŏngsam village, Ch'angnyŏng, Kyŏngnam Province

2. Musical Instruments

PLATE 16 Silver pieces from the tomb of King Munyong. 6th century A.D. *National Museum, Kongju.* See pp.63 - 5

PLATE 17 (top) Two jade flutes. Chosŏn dynasty? Length 55, 47.2 cms, *National Museum, Kyŏngju.* See p.65

(bottom) Jade flute. Chosŏn dynasty. Length 59.2 cms. *National Museum, Kongju*

PLATE 18 Pottery drum of the Koryŏ period. Length 53.8 cms. Diameter of head 19.5 cms. *National Museum, Seoul.* See p.66

PLATE 19 *Shiragi-goto* (Silla *kayagŭm*), detail. 9th century A.D. Length 153.3 cms. *Shōsōin Treasury, Nara, Japan.* (Left) top view (Right) bottom view. See p.65

3. Ceremonial and Official Music

PLATE 20 The lord's procession. Detail from the corridor wall in no.3 tomb, Anak, Hwanghae Province. A.D.357.

PLATE 21 Processional musicians. Detail from the tomb wall at Tŏkhŭngni. A.D.409.

PLATE 22 Processional musicians. Detail from the tomb wall at Susanri. 5th century A.D.

The music played by bands which accompanied processions of officials and troops in early imperial China was called *guchui*, 'banging and blowing'. It was based on popular tunes from home and abroad (Yang *(1)* pp.110-1), and was frequently illustrated on Han tomb decorations. Among the instruments it used were the *xiao* panpipes and a short horn, *jia* (Kor. *ka*), which was often paired with them, a long vertical flute, the mouthorgan, the *jue* (Kor. *kak*) horn, and a number of percussion instruments including several drums, large and small bells and a gong. By the Sui and Tang periods other instruments had arrived from central Asia or been invented in China and were sometimes pressed into service, including the *bili* oboe and a portable version of the *fangxiang* iron slabs. Frequent references to *guchui* (Kor. *koch'wi*) in the *Samguk sagi* indicate that it was familiar to the inhabitants of both Koguryŏ and Paekche.

In 336 A.D. a Chinese official, Dong Shou, emigrated from Liaodong to the neighbouring kingdom of Koguryŏ, where he lived until his death at the age of 69. His tomb was built in the year 357 and decorated, in the Chinese manner and perhaps by Chinese artists, with paintings on the walls of its rooms and corridors. By the time it was discovered in 1949 the paintings were in a poor state of preservation. When new, the processional scene heading north along the eastern wall of the corridor must have provided one of the best illustrations of *guchui* in any early setting, Chinese or Korean (fig.14). In the manner of Korean processions from the earliest times until the Chosŏn dynasty, the ox-drawn carriage of the important personage, presumably Dong Shou himself, comes in the middle of the column and is preceded by one band and followed by another. The front band (Ch. *qianbu*) is on foot and the rear band (Ch. *houbu*) on horseback. 'Front band' may be thought to be a rather grandiose term for a group of three percussion instruments. Two of them are drums, suspended from carrying poles with a central semi-circular arc which raises the upper rim of the drumhead level with the bearers' shoulders, and played by a third person. This drum has been identified by Lee Hye-Ku as the (Ch.) *ganggu* or 'three-man drum', carried in royal processions as late as the Koryŏ dynasty but not illustrated in the later dynasties (Lee H.K.(3) pp. 8-9). It is seen again in wall paintings from the tombs at Tŏkhŭngni (plate 21) and Susanri (plate 22), surmounted on all three occasions by a protective umbrella. The carrying pole of the Tŏkhŭngni drum is furnished with some additional wood- or metal-work which extends the curvature of the arc downwards into almost two thirds of a circle around the drumhead. Not only is this more decorative than the type of support shown on the Anak mural, but it appears to have the additional advantage of helping to fasten the drum more securely. The shaft of the umbrella, straight at Anak, has been given a curve. This drum may be regarded as an intermediary stage between the plain Anak style and that of the Susanri drum. The latter is bigger than those shown in the other two paintings. The carrying pole has been shaped with more attention to style and now forms the top piece of a frame with legs and feet, so that the drum may be stood on the ground. The shaft of the umbrella has also been curved in a more aesthetically pleasing manner. Both the decoration of its head and the three thongs which hang it from the framework anticipate the *chwago* (Cat.no.20), the name of which means 'sitting drum' but which may thus trace its

Fig. 14 The lord's procession. Anak no. 3 tomb

origins back to the processional *ganggu* (Kor. *kanggo*). In the 19th century *ŭigwe* illustrations of this drum (see p.85) the top strut of the frame still retains a similarity with the curved carrying pole of the Koguryŏ period.

At Tŏkhŭngni the *kanggo* is seen in the company of mounted musicians playing the *kak* horn and the small stringed drum, *togo* (Ch. *taogu*), which on Han tomb tiles is sometimes held aloft with one hand by seated musicians while the other holds the *xiao* (fig.15). The *togo* is a smaller version of the *nodo* mentioned on page 84. At Susanri the band also includes the *chŏ* flute and the *kak* horn, the presence of the latter identifying both processions as military. At Anak, the third instrument in the leading band is a bell, hanging from a curved carrying pole and surmounted by an umbrella in the same manner as the drums, and struck on the side by a player with two hammers. Lee Hye-Ku proposes that this bell is the *t'ak,* or *kŭmchong.*

Fig. 15 Han ensemble including a player with *xiao* and *taogu* (second from right)

The rear band at Anak comprises musicians on horseback (fig.16). One plays a *yo* (Ch. *nao*), a small inverted bell without a clapper that is struck on the outside with a hammer. This type of bell originated in China as far back as the Shang dynasty and was still used in Korea for *tangak* as late as the 15th century.[1] To the left of the *yo* player rides a musician whose instrument may be the *ka,* often paired with the panpipes. It is a small, end-blown pipe, evidently without fingerholes since it is held with one hand only, and opening to a small conical bell (Lee, *ibid.*p.11).[2] The illustration suggests that it is slightly curved. Its larger relative the *kak,* the ancestor of the straightened out *nabal* which is a familiar sight in later processions, app-

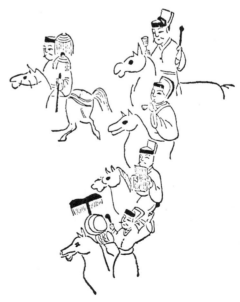

Fig. 16 The rear band at Anak

197

ears in military bands where it would contribute signally to the threatening noise of an approaching army. A medium-sized version is seen in a sixth century tomb mural from Lungkang, held high on the back of a galloping horse (fig. 30(D)). A much longer and heavier example occurs in a fourth century Chinese tomb mural. It is carried on foot and - presumably because of its dimensions - held with the hands wide apart and the curve of the horn sloping down past the player's right hip. It flares only slightly at the bell (fig. 30 (C)). Next to the *ka* player in the rear band rides the *so* player. The panpipes were a popular instrument in Han China and feature prominently in pictures of processional and entertainment music. The final member of the rear band plays a double-bodied drum, one large barrel surmounting a smaller one and fastened by some means to the horse's saddle. This drum, together with those appearing in the Jinan pottery entertainment scene and on the south wall of the front chamber at Anak, show that in both China and Korea the range of drums in use extended beyond those that can yet be identified by distinctive names or compared in more than one illustration.

PLATE 23 Musicians on the west wall of the tomb of Princess Chonghyo, Helongxian, Jilin Province, China. Late 8th/early 9th century A.D.

Not all the people of Koguryŏ were willing to endure Silla rule after the conquest in 668. Some of them, and their descendants, were responsible for founding the new kingdom of Parhae (Ch. Pohai), which enjoyed a relatively untroubled existence for 213 years (713-926) in the region of modern Jilin Province (China) and Hamgyŏng Province (Korea). Diplomatic missions went frequently to China and Chinese influence was naturally strong in the new state. Embassies also went to Japan and were entertained there with music and dance, and the music of Parhae was sufficiently attractive for the Japanese rulers to send courtiers to study it in the second half of the 8th century and to adopt it as a favourite type of music at Nara. There is no evidence to suggest what the music was like, but it was probably within the inherited Koguryŏ and Chinese traditions.

Only one Parhae tomb has so far been discovered, excavated in 1980 at Mount Longtou, Helongxian, Jilin Province.[3] It was the tomb of Princess Chonghyo, fourth daughter of Mun, the third king of Parhae (r.737-793). Built in relatively simple Chinese-Koguryŏ style (fig.17) it was decorated on three sides of the coffin chamber with portraits of the Princess's retainers. The four figures on the west side, 113-117 cms in height, are of musicians, carrying their instruments in protective bags of coloured material. From left to right, the first man holds a sword in his right hand and a long flute over his left shoulder. The second appears to be carrying a set of clappers (*pak*), the third a portable harp *(konghu),* and the fourth a *pip'a* upside down across his shoulder.

PLATE 24 Court audience. Folding screen, late 17th century. Section of panels 3,4,5. *Changdŏk Palace Museum, Seoul*

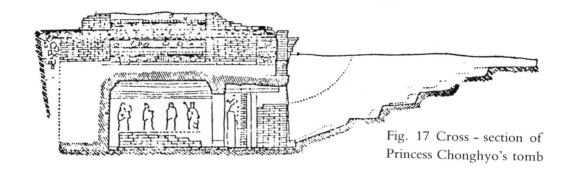

Fig. 17 Cross – section of Princess Chonghyo's tomb

PLATE 25 Detail of the above

PLATE 26 Reception for ministers. Screen panel, 18th century. *National Museum, Seoul*

PLATE 27 Reception for ministers. Screen panel, 18th century. *National Museum, Seoul*

PLATE 28 Court banquet and entertainment scene in the Hall of Benevolent Government. 18th century. 136.1 × 47.6 cms. *National Museum, Seoul*

PLATE 29 Court banquet and entertainment scene, 1902. Panels 3, 4 and 5 of a ten-panel screen. Each panel 196.5 × 60 cms. *National Classical Music Institute, Seoul*

PLATE 30 Panels 6, 7 and 8 of the above

PLATE 31 Detail of panel 3

PLATE 32 Detail of panel 4

PLATE 33 Detail of panel 5

PLATE 34 Detail of panel 6

The varied routine of the court was carried on to the frequent accompaniment of music. It was played on the occasion of state examinations, at archery contests, at banquets for the royal family and elderly officials, at receptions for visiting embassies, and on the seeing off of Korean embassies to China. It preceded the regular monthly meetings between the king and his ministers, and the audiences at which he received their congratulations at New Year, the Winter Solstice and his birthday. Special

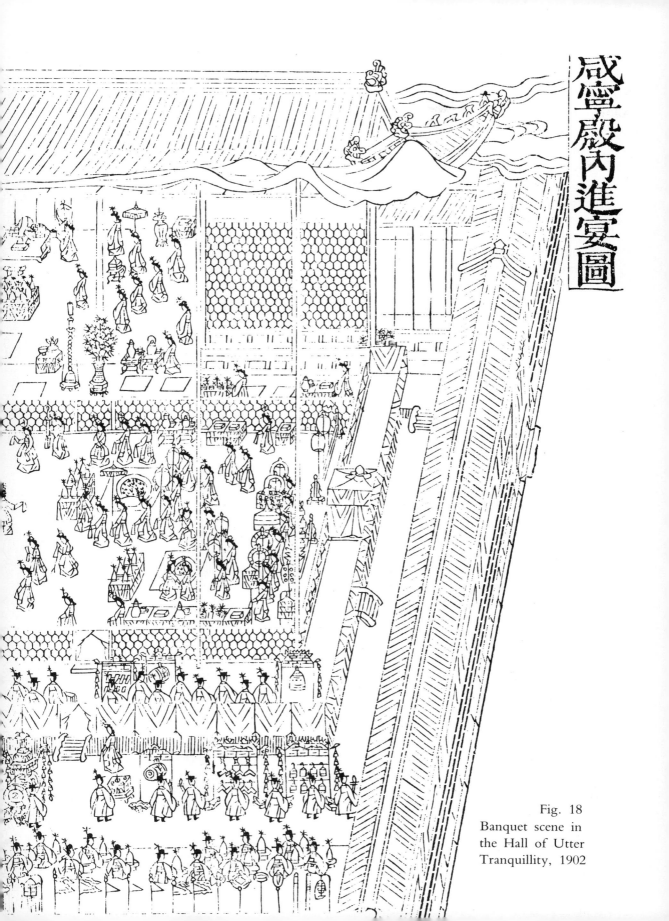

咸寧殿內進宴圖

Fig. 18
Banquet scene in
the Hall of Utter
Tranquillity, 1902

occasions were celebrated on a grand scale. In honour of his father King Kwangmu's birthday in 1902 Prince Sunjong arranged a succession of five banquets in the Tŏksu Palace, three on May 4th and two on the following day. All were accompanied by music and dance. The pattern of entertainment on such occasions had not remained entirely unchanged throughout the Chosŏn dynasty: The Hideyoshi and Manchu invasions and subsequent economies left their mark, as did arguments over propriety which all but led to the replacement of female dancers by boys in the 15th century and did result in the expulsion of masked dance troupes in 1634. However, comparison of accounts of 15th century entertainments with similar ones four hundred years later does indicate an underlying conservatism which perpetuated, for example, among the many dances that were performed, such favourites as the boat dance, the drum dance, the sword dance, the ball-throwing dance, and the four fairies dance. Generally the dancers, who were maintained by the Office of Music, were both male and female. Boys (*mudong*) danced in the presence of government ministers and on other male occasions (known as 'outside banquets'), *kisaeng* at entertainments for female members of the royal family ('inside banquets'). Sometimes exceptions occurred: *Kisaeng* might dance for the king, and on Queen Min's 40th birthday in 1828 all the dancers were male. Boys alone danced at religious ceremonies.

Celebrations often lasted two days. On the first day an orchestra awaited the arrival of the royal procession in the courtyard and a small group of military musicians at the terrace steps. Inside the yellow curtains around the edge of the terrace sat the orchestra that was to accompany the singing and dancing throughout the feast. It was normally arranged in two rows and divided into left and right halves. Dances were performed in a screened off area in front of the hall where the banquet took place. Sometimes, as in 1902, the entire dancing area was enclosed and the guests apparently had to leave the hall to view the entertainment. The musicians would never have been able to see what was taking place.[4] The explanation for this may have to do with the fact that blind players had been employed since ancient times at the Chinese court and were still used in Korea in the 18th century for duties which involved *kisaeng*. By no means all musicians were blind: The post of a court musician was hereditary until the 20th century and this alone would rule out such an improbability. However, it was clearly deemed unwise for the terrace orchestra to cast eyes either on the dancers or the banqueters.

Much of the music that was played in the later part of the dynasty dated back to King Sejong's dance suites and beyond. It included *Pohoja* and *Nagyangch'un*, pieces classified today as *tangak*. Other works are now regarded as *hyangak*, though Condit (3) has postulated Chinese origins for *Yŏmillak* and the original short chant of *Yŏngsan hoesang*, and a central Asian source for *Sujech'ŏn*, which according to the *Koryŏsa* had first been known in Paekche and therefore had an ancient history. Sejong preferred *aak* to *tangak* and it was temporarily used at audiences and banquets during his reign. This practice had been discontinued by the time *Akhak kwebŏm* was compiled in the late

15th century. The constant repetition in rites and entertainments of a very limited number of *tangak* and *hyangak* musical pieces and dances, especially *Yŏmillak* and *Nagyangch'un,* could be accounted for by a belief that the carrying out of perfect actions was of deeper significance and greater interest than the music that accompanied them. A less charitable view is that the attention of the male participants at such occasions was so fixed on the *mudong* and *kisaeng* that they hardly noticed the boring repetition of the same tunes over and over again. Either way, the fact remains that the repertoire was small and the impression is strengthened that court music was little valued *per se.*

Detailed descriptions of the celebrations which took place in fifteen years between 1719 and 1902 were printed in book form, most of them with illustrations. Usually entitled *Chinch'an ŭigwe* ('Rubrics for the conduct of feasts') or *Chinjak ŭigwe* ('Rubrics for the conduct of banquets') these set the standard for all such court entertainment and secular ritual, and ensured continuity of form if not exact repetition of detail over nearly two centuries. The illustrations are not precise portrayals of the scenes they describe : So many participants were involved - musicians, dancers, and the bearers of all manner of banners and decorations - that this could hardly be expected. The terrace orchestra in 1902, for example, comprised 53 persons rather than the 23 shown in fig. 18. The courtyard orchestra had 51 members instead of the eighteen shown in the same picture. Minor discrepancies also occur between the textual diagrams of positional arrangements given in the *ŭigwe* and the number of musicians whose names are all meticulously recorded in the texts. Furthermore, the separate series of pictures which also survive from the 18th to 20th centuries, painted by professional court artists and recording the same events, also appear to under-represent the number of musicians involved. 19th century orchestras were rather larger than their predecessors in the 18th, and on the whole their composition was subject only to minor variation. Numerically, the aerophones constituted the strongest section of the instrumentarium, with *p'iri* and *taegŭm* most prominent in both terrace and courtyard orchestras and one or two *tangjŏk* and *t'ongso* (a small vertical flute with six finger holes and one covered by a membrane) invariably present as well. The *saeng* was introduced in 1828, still with the curved mouthpiece which had disappeared by 1848 (fig.19), and established

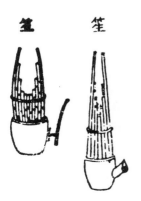

Fig. 19 The *saeng* (left)
in the *ŭigwe* for 1828
and (right) in the *ŭigwe*
for 1848

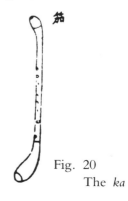

Fig. 20
The *ka*

itself permanently. The strangely shaped *ka* (see note to fig.16) was used from 1828 to 1892 (fig.20), while the *t'aep'yŏngso* made only a brief appearance – its presence in military groups excepted – in 1828 and 1829. Among the wind instruments not used in banquet orchestras were the *so* panpipes and the *hun* ocarina.

Both orchestras possessed a solid body of chordophones. In the front row of the terrace orchestra, which was where the virtuoso players were to be found, were the *kŏmun'go, kayagŭm, ajaeng* and, from 1828 onwards, the *yanggŭm*. *Pip'a* and *haegŭm* were to be seen in both orchestras. Like the *t'aep'yŏngso*, the Chinese 7-stringed zither, *tanggŭm*, was experimented with in 1828 and 1829, but being as soft as the *t'aep'yŏngso* was strident it was presumably found to be just as unsuited to playing in a banqueting ensemble, and was discarded. The single *wŏlgŭm* that was used in the terrace orchestra in 1901 and 1902 may have been similarly outplayed.

The grandest of the idiophones were the *p'yŏnjong* and *p'yŏn'gyŏng,* a pair of which stood on each side of the central divide in the courtyard orchestra. At the inside ends of the front row were the *ch'uk* tub, which took part in the starting phrases, and opposite it the *ŏ* tiger, which helped to indicate the end of a piece. The single bell and chime, *t'ukchong* and *t'ukkyŏng,* which served the same purposes, were introduced to the terrace orchestra in 1902. *Panghyang* were used in both orchestras throughout the entire period covered by the *ŭigwe* series, as they had been since the Koryŏ dynasty.

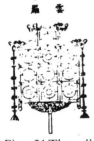

Fig. 21 The *ulla*

By contrast, the appearance of the *ulla* at these entertainments was limited to 1828 and 1829. The *ulla* was a set of ten bronze gong-chimes, suspended in a wooden frame and struck with a hammer (fig.21). It served both as a portable processional instrument, when it was carried in the left hand, and as a pedestal-mounted instrument for court performance. It is now extinct. Three other instruments which were used in the same two years were the small 'bubble' cymbals, *nabara,* the hand-held clapperless bell, *yo,* and the *ching* gong.

The most common membranophone was the *changgo,* of which at least two were always included in both terrace and courtyard orchestras. A similar but heavier drum, the *kalgo,* was sometimes used in the terrace orchestra, as was the vertically mounted frame drum, the *chwago* (see page 84). Three big drums graced the courtyard orchestras, though their usefulness was limited. The *sakko* and the slightly smaller *ŭnggo* were frame-mounted barrel drums and stood in complementary positions, the former in the left half of the orchestra and the latter in the right. Like the tub and the tiger they took part only in the opening and closing phrases of the music. In the midst of the entire orchestra, and dominating it, stood the massive *kŏn'go,* the largest drum ever seen in either Korea or China. Its two heads were approximately 110 cms. in diameter, its body approximately 150 cms. long, and it was surmounted by an ornate wooden pagoda. From the corners of the two topmost storeys protruded the heads of four dragons, long tassels dangling from their mouths, and on the very top stood a white crane, a favourite Korean symbol of long life. This gorgeous instrument, now sadly extinct, was first sent to Korea by Emperor Huizong in 1116, when even in sections it must have added considerably to the fearsome task of transporting that unforgettable gift.

The leader of the courtyard orchestra, signalling the movements with the *pak,* stood adjacent to the *kŏmun'go.* When there were singers, i.e. until 1829 and again in 1901 and 1902, they sat on either side of the centre gangway in the front row of the terrace orchestra.

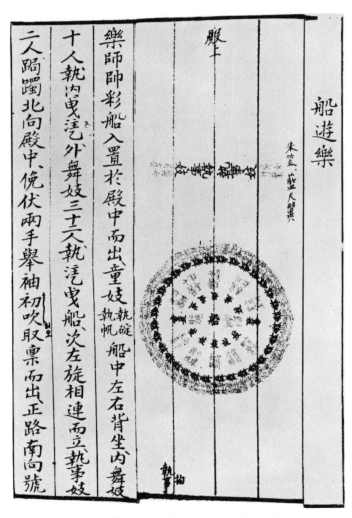

Fig. 22 Choreography for the boat dance

The group of military musicians, those dressed in yellow, played the curved horn, the *t'aep'yŏngso*, the *ching* gong, the *na* gong, the *nabara* small cymbals, the *nabal* horn, the *nagak* conch shell, and a side drum simply referred to as *go* ('drum').

PLATE 35 Kim Hong-do (brush-name Tanwŏn, 1745-?), *Celebrations at the inauguration of the Governor of P'yŏngyang*. Section of a handscroll. 71.2 × 196.9 cms. 18th-19th century. *National Museum, Seoul*

Tanwŏn, though himself a member of the Royal Academy which produced the formal screens seen above, here provides a very different perspective on court entertainment. As the route of the Governor's welcoming procession and the scenes of his eventual reception unroll, the picture is reminiscent of the Chinese documentary scroll style mastered by Zhang Ziduan in the 11th century and seen again in Ch'ŏng Son's *Welcoming Japanese envoys*. The Governor sits on a couch in front of a decorated screen and is watching a masked lion play. The lion is standing on the steps and consists of two players. Its enemy the *tambo* is already inside the hall, where two of the unmasked song and dance girls, *sadang*, are performing. The musical ensemble comprises, from left to right, a *chwago* drum, *changgo*, *p'iri*, *taegŭm* and *haegŭm*. At the end of the line stands the leader with the *pak*. No sign of a sixth player is visible, though comparison of this section of the painting with another section showing the same or a similar ensemble accompanying the sword dance, the ball-throwing dance and the drum dance (Chang (*1*) plate 4) suggests that there should be six. Six was the usual number for a *samhyŏn yukkak* ensemble (see page 249).

To the left of the steps can be seen the props for two more dances, the boat dance (*sŏnyurak*) and the crane dance (*hangmu*). Court dances often focussed their attention on some central object, such as the *chwaggo* in the drum dance or the screen in the ball-throwing dance. In the boat dance, 32 dancers circle around the boat in which two small children sit. After a while the boat is drawn out to 'sea' by six dancers with ropes, while two performers stand guard with sword and bow and arrow. This was a popular dance, dating back at least as far as the Koryŏ dynasty. Its purpose was to invite the blessings of the spirits on the work of the fishing fleets. Lillias Horton, American physician to the Korean queen and wife of the great Presbyterian missionary Horace Underwood, described it as follows in 1904:

> In the grounds before us appeared a pretty boat with wide spread sails, in which were seated some gaily dressed girls. Others now appeared, dancing to slow native music, a stately figure almost in minuet fashion, with waving of floating sleeves and banners. They were evidently the spirits of the wind, and the boat was waiting for the favoring breeze. The music grew quicker, while faster and faster stepped the dancers, more and more swiftly fanning the sails with sleeves, skirts and scarves, till at last the boat slowly moved forward, and with its attendants moved out of sight.[5]

The crane dance can also be traced back to the Koryŏ period and is described in the *Akhak kwebŏm*. At that time it was danced to the music of *Pohŏja,* although by the end of the dynasty this had changed to *Hyangdang kyoju* (or *Ch'aeun sŏnhakchigok*). Two cranes, one blue and the other yellow, enter from the east and west respectively and dance towards the north, where the guest sits. They move to and fro between the north end of the courtyard and an ornamental pond at the south, where two large lotus flowers stand on a platform. At the end of the dance they peck at the flowers and two small girls leap out, symbolising the rebirth of souls in the Amitabha paradise.

PLATE 36 Kim Hong-do, *Party for the elderly at the foot of Songaksan.* 1804 (the year in which Tanwŏn himself attained the auspicious age of 60). 137 × 53.3 cms. *Private collection*

PLATE 37 Detail of the above

PLATE 38 *Banquet for officials.* 1533 A.D. 42.7 × 57.5 cms. *Hong Ik University Museum*

PLATE 39 *Entertainment at a meeting of the Society for the Elderly and Brave.* 1585 A.D. 40.1 × 59.4 cms. *Seoul National University Museum*

PLATE 40 *Banquet for the elderly given by Yi Wŏn-ik.* 1623 A.D. *National Museum, Seoul*

PLATE 41 *Royal banquet for the Society of the Elderly,* given in 1719. Picture dated 1730 A.D. 36 × 52 cms. *Hoam Museum of Fine Arts*

PLATE 42 Detail of the above

PLATE 43 *Members' private banquet following the meeting of the Society of the Elderly.* 1720 A.D. 36 × 52 cms. *Hoam Museum of Fine Arts*

PLATE 44 *Banquet given by the royal family.* 1744 A.D. 134.5 × 64 cms. *Seoul National University Museum*

One of the strongest and most practical injunctions of Confucianism concerned the care of parents and the elderly. Korean monarchs took it very seriously, and both Koryŏ and Chosŏn dynastic records contain many references to edicts commanding provincial authorities to make donations of food and clothing to people of seventy and eighty years and over. The caption to a picture in an 18th century book showing *kisaeng* playing *kayagŭm* music for the entertainment of the elderly on Cheju Island says that 183 octogenarians, 23 nonogenarians, and three centenarians were present! [6] The court itself set a good example. In 1795 75,145 people were invited to celebrate the Dowager Queen's birthday.

In 1394 King T'aejo had founded the Office of the Venerable Aged, *Kiroso* (*Kisa* for short), with the purpose of honouring officials of upper second rank who had attained the age of seventy. Reigning kings were allowed to join at the age of sixty and three had themselves elected at even younger ages, Sukchong at 59 in 1719, Yŏngjo at 51 in 1744, and Kojong at 51 in 1902. Between 1475 and the early 17th century the organisation was renamed the Society for the Elderly and Brave (*Kiyonghoe*). Twice a year the Board of Rites was required to arrange entertainments for the members. The king gave a banquet in the Poje Pavilion, with music consisting of *hyangak* (usually *Yŏmillak*) and *aak* (*Hyuanjigok*, one of Zhu Xi's reconstructed pieces), and on the following day the members held a private meeting. According to *Akhak kwebŏm* they played pitchpot, *tuho*, with the incentive of drink and the repeated playing of *Nagyang-ch'un*. Pitchpot was an ancient Chinese ritual game revived in Korea after the receipt of the gift of instruments in 1116. Nie Chongi's *San li tu* (996 A.D.) illustrates the instruments that were played during its performance in China, including the bells and chimes. Details of the Korean accompaniment are found in *Akhak kwebŏm*. The music belonged to *soak* ('bestowed music'), of which there were four classes, the first comprising 10 musicians and 20 *kisaeng*, the second 10 musicians and 15 *kisaeng*, the third 7 musicians and 10 *kisaeng*, and the fourth 5 musicians and 6 *kisaeng* (Lee H.K. (6) vol.1 p.111). At a meeting of the Society in 1564 *soak* of the fourth class was performed by an ensemble comprising *tangp'iri*, *changgo*, *taegŭm*, *kŏmun'go* and *haegŭm*, with six *kisaeng* (Lee H.K.(5), frontispiece). Plate 39 shows *soak* of the second class, with 15 *kisaeng*, ten musicians (playing, from left to right, *taegŭm*, drum, *tangpip'a*, *haegŭm*, *pak*, *taegŭm*, *kŏmun'go*, *changgo*, *changgo* and *p'iri*) and a leader seated to the left of the band. In plates 41 and 43 no *kisaeng* are shown and entertainment is provided by five masked dancers. In 1623 their accompaniment consists of eleven musicians and a leader, and the instruments include the bells and chimes. In 1719, the year in which King Sukchong was made a member of the *Kisa* and the subject of plates 41 and 42, the *Ch'ŏyong* masked dance was performed both at the banquet given by the King himself on 17th April and at the members' private banquet on the following day. The orchestra on the first of these occasions was larger than those prescribed for *soak*, no doubt reflecting the King's personal interest in the proceedings. Once again the bells and chimes are present, together with other instruments of the *aak* tradition such as the *ch'uk* tub, two large suspended barrel drums, and the huge *kŏn'go*. Lined up in front of them are four *taegŭm*, two *p'iri*, four *changgo*, and in front of these four *tangpip'a*, four *haegŭm*, two *kayagŭm* and one *kyobanggo* drum. At the private banquet the bells, chimes, barrel drums, *kŏn'go*, *ch'uk* and *kayagŭm* have disappeared, still leaving a large ensemble of nineteen which is obviously delighting the onlookers. The inscription on the picture of the banquet given in 1744 (plate 44) says that the music is *soak*, although the number of performers depicted, namely eleven musicians, six *kisaeng* and a leader, does not conform to any of the four classes defined in *Akhak kwebŏm*.

The *Ch'ŏyong* dance sequence, a favourite court entertainment which had been part of the repertoire as far back as the 15th century, was performed by five men or boys wearing brocaded silk costumes and masks, which from their prominent facial features and hair seem to have had a foreign origin. Each of the five was dressed in a different colour, red representing south, black north, blue east, white west and yellow centre. After a series of solos, yellow danced with each of the remaining four colours in turn, before a group dance by all five presaged the end of the entertainment. The origins of the dance are buried in the Three Kingdoms period and are probably associated with the *Obang sinjangmu* ('Dance of the gods of the five directions') and the *Ogwangdae* mask play, which like the *Ch'ŏyong* dance was used as an act of exorcism on New Year's Eve and thus, like so many features of Korean music and dance, indicates a shamanist connection. The story of Ch'ŏyong himself, son of the Dragon of the Eastern Sea and son-in-law of the Silla King Hŏn'gang (r.875-886), has a number of variants. In the Chosŏn dynasty the five dancers sang a version of Ch'ŏyong's song which had appeared in the *Samguk yusa* (13th century):

> Under the moonlight of the Eastern Capital
> I revelled late into the night.
> When I came home and entered my bedroom
> I saw four legs.
> Two legs were mine,
> Whose were the other two?
> The person underneath was mine,
> But whose body was taking her?
> What should I do?

What he did do in fact was to forgive his wife's seducer, the God of Sickness, who in gratitude promised to avoid any household displaying Ch'ŏyong's portrait on the doorpost. A different legend helps to account for the ugly masks used in the dance. It tells of a minstrel named Ch'ŏyong whose strange looks, conduct and ability to prophesy brought him to the attention on the Silla court. One night there appeared with him four exceptionally ugly men foretelling the fall of the Silla kingdom. The court ignored their warnings and continued in its carefree over-indulgence, until it no longer commanded the respect of its most powerful subjects and fell. Thereafter Ch'ŏyong was regarded as the patron deity of masked dancers, while in later generations the court evidently felt that the story, despite its explicit sexuality, provided a sufficiently salutary lesson to warrant regular telling.

PLATE 45 *King Chŏngjo's visit to his father's tomb.* Panel of a screen painting. 149.8 × 64.5 cms. *Changdŏk Palace Museum, Seoul*

PLATE 46 Detail of the above

PLATE 47 *King Chŏngjo's visit to his father's tomb.* Detail from a horizontal handscroll 1811 A.D. 1,536×36.6 cms. *Seoul National University Library*

NOTES TO THE PLATES

Among Korean exemplars of filial piety few are better known than King Chŏngjo (1776-1800). Coming to the throne prematurely at the age of ten as the result of his father's murder by his grandfather, King Yŏngjo, he continually sought to expunge the sense of familial guilt by establishing his father in as close a position of honour as possible to the one he would have occupied as a deceased king.[7] He gave him the title of Crown Prince Changho or "King" Changjo, and when in 1776 he had a temple, Kyŏngmogung, built for him in the grounds of the Changdŏk Palace, officials were ordered to draw up ceremonial rites that stopped only just short of those befitting a king. In 1789 he had his father's body moved from an obscure grave to a more fitting site outside Suwŏn, 51 kilometres south of Seoul. Suwŏn was an attractive city much favoured by Chŏngjo, who fortified and developed it between 1794 and 1796 and made it one of the most important provincial centres in Korea. Near the tomb mound he had a Buddhist temple, Yŏngjusa, built which became the flourishing headquarters of the official Chogye-jong sect. The King made frequent visits to the tomb and his devotional duties were recorded by court artists. Scenes of the royal procession to Suwŏn were favourite subjects for copyists, and the eight-panel screen preserved at the Changdŏk Palace includes a series of *ŭigwe* paintings showing rites, audiences and entertainments at the Kyŏngmogung. In portraying the court on the march, early nineteenth century artists either managed to convey the sense of occasion, in which case the ability to combine this with total accuracy of detail seems to have eluded them, or they opted for the latter and made no attempt to suggest the crowds, the movement and the atmosphere in the surrounding countryside. Thus in panel 2 of the screen - the scene as the procession crowds over the river bridge at Suwŏn - only a small band and a few drummers can be seen, while in panel 3, depicting the arrival of the court in the tomb area, no musicians at all are visible. We know from literary sources, however, that when the King made this excursion his palanquin was preceded by a band consisting of gongs, *nagak* conch shells, *nabal* horns, cymbals, *t'aep'yŏngso* and drums, and followed by another including *taegŭm*, *haegŭm*, *p'iri* and *changgo*. By contrast, the long scroll seen in plate 47 provides a precise record of the royal bands, while clearly making no attempt at verisimilitude.

Only two pieces of military processional music still survive, instrumented nowadays for *t'aep'yŏngso*, *nabal*, conch shell, gong, cymbals and barrel drum (*yonggo*). Early in the Chosŏn dynasty, royal processional bands were larger and may have included portable versions of the *panghyang*, *ulla*, *tangpip'a*, *tangjŏk* and *t'ongso*, in addition to the instruments already mentioned.

PLATE 48 attr. Ch'ŏng Son (brush-name Kyomjae, 1676 - 1759), *Greeting Japanese envoys at Dongnae*. Detail of a painting on ten screen panels, each 85 × 46 cms. *National Museum, Seoul*

PLATE 49 Further detail of the above

PLATE 50 Further detail of the above

PLATE 51 Anon., *Korean envoys' procession to Japan*. 1636 A.D. Detail of a horizontal scroll. 30.7 × 595 cms. *National Museum, Seoul*

PLATE 52 Further detail of the above

Envoys had been coming and going between Korea and Japan since the Three Kingdoms period. The Koreans had learned the correct formation of a processional band from the Chinese, namely a larger group of noisier instruments (called the *ch'wita,* 'blowing and banging' band) in front of the official's chair and a smaller, more restrained one (called *seak,* 'fine music') behind it. The *Sui shu* described the composition of front and rear bands in the 6th-7th centuries as follows:

Front: large drum, small drum, war drum, long horn, medium horn, shoulder-pole drum (*ganggu*), cymbals;

Rear: *nao* (clapperless handbell), panpipes, *jia* horn, *jiegu* drum, oboe, horizontal flute, horn (*SS* 8, p.160).[8]

More than a thousand years later the formational principle was still the same. The leading band was intent on making a loud noise, either to frighten the enemy or to warn bystanders of an official's approach: The rear band was more melodious.

Twelve Korean cultural missions are recorded between the years 1607 and 1811, travelling via Tsushima Island at the invitation of the Tokugawa government to celebrate the accession of a new Shōgun.[9] The smallest numbered 300 persons (1624 A.D.) and the largest 500 (1711 A.D.). Officials, secretaries, actors, dancers and artists were included in the retinue, with approximately fifty musicians. The Toshuku at Nikko preserves a *ch'uk* tub and an *ŏ* tiger which formed part of the gift of instruments sent by King Hyojong with the 1655 mission to commemorate the shrine's founder, the first Tokugawa Shōgun. The passing of the noisy, colourful troupes made a deep impression on the Japanese villagers, and both Korean and Japanese artists recorded them on horizontal scrolls. The front bands included the familiar *t'aep'yŏngso, nabal,* cymbals, conch shells and drums; amongst the rear bands were a greater variety of instruments, including the large *sul* zither, the *haegŭm* and *chŏ* horizontal flute.

When a Japanese envoy visited Korea it was again the Koreans who provided the accompanying musical entourage. Ch'ŏng Son's ten-panel screen records the initial stages of one such visit, showing the magistrate at Dongnae on his way to greet his guest at the port of Pusan, the trip to the official guest house at Dongnae, and the entertainment provided there for the envoy. On panels 4 and 5 six musicians precede the magistrate's palanquin playing *changgo* and *puk, p'iri* and *tanso, taegŭm* and *haegŭm.* On panel 7, the group of musicians heading the procession and about to pass through the gateway play two conch shells, two *nabal,* two *t'aep'yŏngso,* two cymbals, three gongs, two *ulla* and two *puk.* Panels 9 and 10 show the envoy being entertained by *kisaeng* and eight musicians. In addition to the normal *samhyŏn yukkak* ensemble a large suspended gong is visible.

PLATE 53 After Kim Tŭk-sin (brush-name Kungjae, 1754-1822). *Playing music for Guo Fenyang*. Detail of a screen panel 614 × 141.6 cms. *Private Collection*

Kungjae was a member of the Academy, well known as a figure painter and adept at painting both in a Chinese style and in the Korean *genre* form. The composition of *Playing music for Guo Fenyang* strongly recalls that of the complex Sui and Tang dynasty paintings of the Buddhist heavens found at Dunhuang and later copied by Korean artists, which were doubtless based on Chinese court scenes. The Tang nobleman Guo Fenyang occupies the central position – that of the Amitabha Buddha on so many murals – and is surrounded by a multitude of male and female attendants and acolytes. Above his head the curling branches of the pine trees are reminiscent of the swirls of cloud through which devas used to fly on wispy ribbons. The pattern of the entertainment taking place before him, provided by a dancer whirling around a mat placed between two groups of female musicians, is frequently seen in Tang murals, the only difference being that the earlier Chinese orchestras were usually seated.[10] Both left and right halves of Kungjae's orchestra consist of eight girls. Their instruments include some of those that were generally present in Tang orchestras such as the four-stringed lute, the mouthorgan, and both vertical and horizontal flutes. Of special interest is the long horn, similar in shape to that seen in plate 59, and the two miniature sets of gong-chimes, each with only four gongs instead of the ten which formed the complete *ulla*. Missing from the ensemble are two instruments that appear frequntly in pictures of Tang orchestras accompanying dancers, the harp and the panpipes. Neither of these had any musical prominence in 18th century Korea.

A 19th century copy of this picture on screen panels is in the John W. Grieder collection in Dalton, Pennsylvania. According to its title, the entertainment is there being provided for the Tang General Gui Zi'i.

PLATE 54 attr. Kim Hong-do, *Scenes from the life of Hong I-sang: procession of the newly successful graduate*. 1781 A.D. Screen panel. 122.7 × 47.9 cms. *National Museum, Seoul*

PLATE 55 Anon., *Procession of the newly successful graduate*. 19th century. Detail of a screen panel. 91.5 × 42 cms. *Seoul National University Museum*

PLATE 56 *Procession of the newly appointed magistrate*. Further panel of the above

The six most important occasions in the life of a Korean man were his first birthday, his coming of age, his marriage, the attainment of his *chinsa* degree, the appointment to his first official post, and his sixtieth birthday. Pictures of these auspicious events decorated screens which were known (like the Buddhist temple paintings discussed below) as *p'yŏngsaengdo*. Music appears on only two panels of

Tanwŏn's screen honouring the career of Hong I-sang and on the 19th century copy of it shown in plates 55 and 56. A six-piece band precedes the graduate in plates 54 and 55. It consists of one *haegŭm,* one *taegŭm,* two *p'iri,* one *changgo,* and one heavier drum carried on a shoulder-pole. The small cartouches in Tanwŏn's picture are not uncommon in Korean popular art. Here they name the instruments and other elements in the procession, as well as drawing attention to the watching bystanders. The magistrate's procession, larger and grander though it may be, contains only four musicians, two with drums, one with a *t'aep'yŏngso* and one with a pair of cymbals.

PLATE 57 Anon., *View of P'yŏngyang Castle.* 19th century. Screen panels, each 131 × 39 cms. *Seoul National University Museum*

PLATE 58 Detail of the above

PLATE 59 Detail of the above

Two groups of musicians appear in the central panels of this screen. Inside the castle walls the governor's chair passes the Bell Tower on its way to the main gate to the accompaniment of two horns and a gong. A procession moves across the bottom of the picture. In its band we can see, from right to left, two horns with tulip-shaped bells reminiscent of the horn depicted in plate 53, two conch shells, two drums, two cymbals, two gongs, two *ulla* with nine gongs, and two medium-length horns with flared bells.

PLATE 60 Anon., *Hunting scene.* 19th century? Detail of a screen panel. *Emille Museum*

Scenes of equestrian figures dressed in nomadic costume hunting tigers, bears and deer were popular for decorating military headquarters, soldiers' living apartments etc. The horn shown in this picture is quite distinct from the curved horns with flared bells that appear in earlier mural paintings, and from the shorter *t'aep'yŏngso* and the longer *nabal* that are both familiar in later processions. A similar instrument is seen in plate 53.

4. Religious Music

A. HUMAN MUSICIANS

PLATE 61 Anon., *Portrait of Pak Yŏn and his wife.* 59.5 × 34.5 cms. *National Classical Music Institute, Seoul*

PLATE 62 The sacrifice at the Royal Ancestral Shrine. Detail of a screen painting. 19th century. *Chongmyo Palace Museum, Seoul*

It is fitting that the section on religious music should begin with a tribute to the man who is renowned as one of Korea's greatest musicologists, the scholar whose devotion and contributions to the cause of Confucian ritual music must have appeared to his contemporaries to have done as much as anything in King Sejong's progressive and exciting reign to ensure the vital balance in the affairs of heaven and earth.

Pak Yŏn's achievements were the fruits of experience and maturity. Though he had had an early appointment in the Hall of Worthies - a department developed by King Sejong to foster the spirit of intellectual enquiry which contributed to advances in medicine, music, cartography, astronomy, and the invention of *han'gŭl* - it was not until he was 47 years of age that we hear of the first of his long series of memorials devoted to the reform of court music. Over the next thirty years the Veritable Annals (*Sejong sillok*) record more than forty of his proposals on music, many of them to do with the manufacture and use of instruments and all but a few approved by the King. In the second half of his career he rose from being Third Tutor in the Crown Prince's Tutorial Office, a post of Upper Fifth rank, to the exalted position of a Senior Magistrate in the provincial administration (Upper Second rank).

Strongly influenced by the neo-Confucian ethics of the early 15th century, Pak developed a pre-occupation about the need for purity in music. His first recorded memorial asked for permission to collect music books from all over the country.[11] This task probably stood him in good stead some years later when King Sejong conceived the idea of the *Dragons ascending* song-cycle. For the moment, it helped to crystallise his views on the need to clean up music at court, not only to rid it of the improper expressions of love and Buddhist ideology, but also to correct its theory and the way it was performed. In the same spirit, he is said to have warned his descendants about the dangers of *samhyŏn yukkak,* by which he presumably meant contemporary popular music, and thus expressed the age-old concern of Korean and Chinese musicologists about the corrupting influence of impure, modern music.

It was in 1426 that Pak first expressed an interest in revising the court's *aak.* This seems to have been occasioned by the discovery of stone suitable for making a Korean set of chimes *(p'yŏn' gyŏng).* Only one set of those sent from China in 1116 still survived, and although others had ben sent by the Hongwu and Yongle Emperors they were not thought to be of such good quality. Pak's first move was to construct a set of pitch-pipes for the tuning of the new chimes, but although he made these according to ancient Chinese specifications the result was out of tune with the Song chimes. Pak Yŏn's nerve faltered, and rather than embark on the awkward and embarrassing task of retuning the Chinese instruments he scrapped his own pitch-pipes and tuned the new stones in accordance with the existing ones. His conviction about the need to reform ritual music, however, was undiminished, and in the autumn of 1430 King Sejong himself was constrained to read books on the theory of music, after which he commanded the First Counsellor of the Hall of Worthies and author of the *Koryŏsa,* Chŏng In-ji, together with Pak Yŏn and others, to "put ancient music in proper order". Perhaps the King's decision had something to do with the fact that he had already received 23 memorials that year from Pak Yŏn on the subject. Within three months the scholars had produced the fruits of their labours, a new transcription of music for sacrificial and royal audience rites based on six tunes by the Song dynasty Chinese scholar Zhu Xi and twelve by the Yuan dynasty musician Lin Yu (Provine (1)). It was given its first performance the following month, the first of 1431. Chŏng In-ji's Introduction to the *Notations of ceremonial music,* in which this music is recorded, not unnaturally gives the King credit for initiating the research after his own investigations in September 1430. It is clear, however, that it had been under way for some time, and that the moving spirit behind it was Pak Yŏn.

Throughout the 1430s and 1440s Pak rose steadily in rank. He continued to have new instruments made for *aak,* which replaced *tangak* at court audiences and was added to *tangak* and *hyangak* at royal banquets. He had more boy dancers recruited and new costumes designed for them. Most important of all, he continued to work on the compilation of purified ceremonial music, including new versions of *Yŏmillak* and *Pot'aep'yŏng,* and he assisted in the creation of the *Dragons ascending to the heavens* (1447).

Solid indeed must Pak Yŏn's achievements have seemed by the time he retired in 1445. He was then 77 years old and had just three more years to live. The history of music in China, however, was already strewn with the discarded efforts of reformers who were eventually deemed to have failed in their attempts to do the impossible, create music of such purity that its effects on the fortunes of the empire were incontrovertibly recognised. Pak Yŏn was luckier than some, for his efforts were not overturned during his own lifetime and his reputation subsequently grew rather than diminished. By the end of the 15th century, however, the 'modernists' had reasserted themselves. The women against whose presence in banquet entertainments at court Pak had memorialised were still dancing at court. *Aak* had been replaced again by *tangak* and *hyangak* at audiences and banquets and even at the Royal Ancestral Shrine. *Samhyŏn yukkak* was still delighting all classes of society.

How, then, should we assess Pak Yŏn's contribution to the history of Korean music? Dour and unattractive though he may seem as a person, his enthusiasm for his cause did perhaps provide the object of it - ritual and ceremonial music - with strength to survive the traumatic events that were soon to follow. His passionate concern about the proper use of ancient instruments may have assisted their continued use and manufacture in Korea. Disillusioned though he might ultimately have been at the fate of his *aak*, some of the grandest pieces of *hyangak* which he had a hand in creating are still in frequent use nearly five hundred years later. Finally, it is possible that the subject of his very first memorial, the collection of materials for the compilation of a new standard treatise on musical theory and practice, might have been the inspiration behind King Songjong's commissioning of just such a work in 1492, *Akhak kwebŏm*. Major credit for the book goes, of course, to Sŏng Hyŏn, but the concept was indeed worthy of Pak Yŏn.

* * * * *

Buddhism brought with it beliefs and practices which, in the course of time, inspired a number of recurrent artistic themes incorporating musical elements. Three of these are of human subjects whilst three more - the flying devas, the scenes of Paradise, and the *pip'a*-playing King of the East - belong to the realms of the divine and are discussed in section B below. The three which represent human situations are 'Scenes from the life of Buddha', 'Scenes from daily life', and the *simudo* ('oxherd paintings') series of Sŏn pictures.

Fig. 23 Detail from a scene in the life
of Buddha. Sŏngnamsa

PLATE 63 Scene from the life of Buddha. Detail from a wall painting in the Yŏngsan Hall, T'ongdosa. 18th century

Scenes from the life of Buddha provided artists with two particular opportunities to portray music. The first lay in the depiction of his early life. Prince Sakyamuni himself was a gifted musician, and his appreciation of music might be shown with illustrations of performances by instrumentalists and dancers. The second referred to the temptations that beset him following his renunciation of worldly pleasures, and naturally included the sight and sound of the entertainment that he had previously enjoyed. In addition to these two, other scenes of his birth, noble upbringing, teaching, suffering and death gave ample scope for the inclusion of passing musical references. Sometimes this series of pictures adorned the outside walls of a temple building, as it does at Sŏngnamsa, where a divine musician comforts the suffering Sakyamuni with a strangely shaped *ohyŏn* lute (fig.23). The series in the small, dark, but sumptuously decorated Yŏngsan Hall at T'ongdosa is one of the most complete. Music does not feature prominently in it, however, and the dimensions of the *kayagŭm* held by the attendant in this plate suggest that the artist was not concerned with the accuracy of musical detail. As in religious art the world over, the purpose of those who painted the life of Buddha was didactic rather than descriptive, and in recent centuries especially the portrayal of musical instruments in Buddhist temples has been rather impressionistic.

PLATE 64 Scenes from daily life: A procession towards the Buddhist temple. Detail from a large wall picture in the Great Buddha Hall, Pang'wŏnsa, Seoul. 20th century

PLATE 65 Monks chanting sutras. Further detail from the above picture

PLATE 66 Scenes from daily life: Monks' cymbal dance. Detail from a wall picture in the main hall of Yŏngamsa, Seoul. 1865 A.D.

PLATE 67 Scenes from daily life: Monks with a large drum. Detail from a wall picture in the Great Buddha Hall, Yŏngjusa, Suwŏn. 18th century

PLATE 68 Shaman and musicians. Further detail from the above picture

PLATE 69 Scenes from daily life: Shaman and musicians. Detail from a wall picture preserved at Hoam Museum of Fine Arts. 19th century

P'yŏngsaengdo 'Pictures of daily life' is the name given to the large painting which may be found on either the left or the right wall of the main building in a Buddhist temple, showing the role played by the church in the community and the promise of continued life in another existence. In the centre and near the top of the picture, immediately below the realm of the Buddha, is the temple itself. To the left of it a group of monks perform dances to the accompaniment of gongs, cymbals and drums. Other monks may be chanting sutras to the left or right of the temple entrance as a procession, with its leading band of *nabal,* conch shells and drums, approaches the gateway. To the right of the temple stand a magistrate and his attendants, sometimes with a small boy playing a flute but generally with no other musicians. Below centre on the left side of the picture, near the market scenes, a small band of *kwangdae* musicians play for a tightrope walker, and below them a shaman dances to the accompaniment of her own two-man ensemble. Her invariable inclusion in this Buddhist picture, albeit at the bottom in keeping with her lowly social status, is recognition of the frequent interaction of shamanist and Buddhist functions in Korean society. On the right hand side of the picture groups of *kwangdae* entertainers may appear, not far from the unfortunate miscreants undergoing alarming punishments as ordered by the magistrate. In and around all these vignettes of village life move additional monks and peasants, watching and participating and completing a lively and colourful picture in a folk art branch of the *genre* tradition. The amount and nature of the detail in the picture, and its style, might vary according to its age, but the basic pattern and constituent scenes have remained consistent at least from the 18th to the 20th centuries.[12]

PLATE 70 Sin Yun-bok (brush-name Hyewŏn, 1758–c. 1818), *Shaman with musicians.* Album leaf. 35.2 × 28.3 cms. *Kansong Museum of Fine Arts, Seoul*

PLATE 71 Sin Yun-bok, *Buddhist beggar with large drum.* Album leaf. 35.2 × 28.3 cms. *Kansong Museum of Fine Arts, Seoul*

PLATE 72 *Oxherd playing a flute.* One of an anonymous series of *simudo* paintings on the exterior rear wall of the Great Buddha Hall, Chogyesa, Seoul. Early 20th century

One of the best known subjects in the whole of east Asian art is the oxherd riding on the back of his beast and playing a transverse flute. It has been painted over and over again by leading masters and humble folk artists alike, and has been the inspiration for sculptors in bronze and wood and bone. In Korean Buddhist art it is frequently seen as one of the sets of pictures which originated with the Chan (Kor. *Sŏn,* Japanese *Zen*) sect in China, depicting the boy's gradual enlightenment through five to ten stages. Having found and tethered the ox he then rides it home, his awareness of physical impermanence and spiritual reality growing and symbolised by the changing colour of the ox from brown to white, until finally boy and ox together disappear into a dazzling invisibility. Music is not the prime catalyist to his transfiguration but it is a perfect foil to it. Nothing epitomizes the calm spirit of Buddhist meditation better than the soft, contemplative tone of the *taegŭm.* It is no coincidence that monks in *p'yŏng-saengdo* pictures, as well as attendants upon the Daoist Immortals, are often depicted with this flute, nor that Korean literature describes it as the instrument of the fairies.

B. DIVINE MUSICIANS

1) DEVAS

PLATE 73 Deva playing a horn. Detail of a mural from the Tomb of the Dancers, Tonggou, nr. Jian, Jilin, Province, China. 5th-6th century A.D.

PLATE 74 Four musicians from the side of a stone Amitabha Trinity from Piamsa. 673 A.D. 43 × 26.7 cms. *National Museum, Seoul.* Top left: *so.* Top right: horizontal flute (*chŏ*). Bottom left: *saenghwang.* Bottom right: bent-necked *pip'a*

PLATE 75 Four musicians from the opposite side of the above stone. Top left: waist drum (*yogo*). Top right: waist drum (*yogo*). Bottom left: *kŏmun'go.* Bottom right: *changjŏk*

PLATE 76 Musicians on four stones from a pedestal of the Silla period. Height c.60 cms. *National Museum, Kyŏngju.* A: *saenghwang.* B: horizontal flute. C: *pip'a.* D: small cymbals

PLATE 77 One of twelve musicians from the side of a 9th century granite pagoda at Hwaŏmsa, Kurye, Cholla Namdo, playing the *saenghwang.* Pagoda height 5.54 m. Figure approx. 45 cms

PLATE 78 Two of six musicians from the side of the memorial pagoda to the monk Chi Jung. 904 A.D. Height of pagoda 3.41 m. Figures approx. 33 cms. Pongamsa, Mun'gyŏng, Kyŏngsan Pukto. A: *pip'a.* B: *p'iri*

PLATE 79 Four of eight musicians from the sides of a Koryŏ period pagoda. Pagoda height 2.39 m. Figures c.33 cms. *National Kyŏngbok University Museum.* A: *ohyŏn pip'a.* B: *saenghwang.* C: *konghu.* D: *chŏ*

PLATE 80 Bronze bell. 725 A.D. Sangwŏnsa, Kangwŏn Province. Height 167 cms., diameter at mouth 91 cms

PLATE 81 Detail of the above: Deva musicians playing the *konghu* (left) and the *saenghwang* (right)

PLATE 82 Moulded relief of a musician playing the *pip'a* on the side of a Silla period bell. Probably 9th century. Height 95.25 cms. *National Museum, Kongju*

PLATE 83 Deva musician playing the small cymbals. Figure from the opposite side of the above bell

PLATE 84 Moulded relief of musicians playing a *saenghwang* and a flute on the side of a Silla bell. 9th century. H. 99 cms., diameter 102 cms. *Tongguk University Museum*

PLATE 85 Bronze deva playing a flute (now missing). 8th century. H. 11.8 cms *National Museum, Seoul*

PLATE 86 Bronze sarira case decorated with figures of musicians and dancers. 628 A.D. H.15 cms. From Kamŭnsa. *National Museum, Seoul*

PLATE 87 Figures of four musicians from the corners of the above sarira case. A : waist drum *(yogo).* B : small cymbals. C : horizontal flute *(chǒ).* D : phoenix-head *pip'a*

PLATE 88 Tiny metal openwork figure of a deva playing a flute. Silla period. H. c.3 cms. *National Museum, Kyǒngju*

PLATE 89 Musician playing a *saenghwang*. Wood carving on an altar frontal. 18th century. Pǒmǒsa, Pusan

PLATE 90 Musician playing a drum. Exterior wall painting. 18th century. Pǒmǒsa, Pusan

PLATE 91 Musician playing a drum. Ceiling painting. 19th century. Kapsa, Kongju

PLATE 92 Musician playing the *nabal*. Ceiling painting. 19th century. Songgwangsa, Chonju

PLATE 93 Musician carrying a *haegŭm*. Ceiling painting. Early 20th century. Pǒmǒsa, Pusan

PLATE 94 Musicians playing a *kayagŭm* (left) and a vertical flute. Exterior wall painting on the Gate of the Heavenly Kings, T'ongdosa, Kyǒngsang Namdo. 19th century

Devas were flying creatures born in the Pure Land of Amitabha Buddha to wait upon Buddha and to entertain him. Goddesses of fragrance and music, they were believed to appear as Buddha preached on the Dharma, filling the atmosphere with music and flowers. Wingless, they flew by means of the flowing belts and ribbons which adorned their dress, but after the translation into Chinese in the early 5th century of a story from the *Sudharma-pundarika Sutra,* relating how the devas had offered their upper garments to Buddha, they were often depicted as naked from the waist upwards. They possessed the power of invisibility, and in caves 172 and 217 at Dunhuang be-ribboned instruments can be seen flying through the sky as if of their own accord.[13] In Korea, where no murals survive which are either contemporary or in any way comparable with those of Dunhuang, no such extravagant flights of fancy are to be seen, although devas do sometimes ride on the backs of cranes.

Surviving illustrations of Korean devas fall mainly into three categories, (i) those to be found in tomb murals from the kingdom of Koguryŏ; (ii) those carved on stone monuments or moulded on bronze bells, mostly of the Silla and Koryŏ periods; (iii) those painted on the walls and ceilings of temple buildings, mostly of the late Chosŏn dynasty and early 20th century. Though far less numerous and varied in appearance and activity than their Chinese cousins, they nevertheless play a range of musical instruments. These cannot constitute evidence about the actual performance of Buddhist music, but they do help to amplify the written evidence about the general state of musical appreciation in earlier periods.

(i) *Koguryŏ tomb murals.* Six instruments used by devas on early wall paintings deserve special attention:

1. The *wanham* (Ch. *yuanxian*). This was the oldest of the Chinese lutes, probably pre-dating the arrival of the *pipa* in east Asia and sometimes known as the *qin pipa*.

Fig. 24 Yuan Xian playing the Chinese lute

Fig. 25 Two devas playing
the *wanham*, Chang
Chuan no 1 tomb

From the mid-Tang period it was also called the 'moon zither' (*yueqin*, Kor. *wŏlgŭm*), after the round face of its bowl. Its neck was narrow and long, and according to Fu Xuan (217-278)'s *Pipa fu* it had twelve frets and four strings. Its common name was derived from that of one of the Seven Sages of the Bamboo Grove, Yuan Xian, who was a virtuoso player and is often pictured with it. The Seven Sages held their famous meetings in China between 245 and 255 A.D. On an Eastern Jin tile decoration he is shown using a plectrum to pluck its strings (fig.24). The player often held the neck in his left hand parallel to the ground ⬙ but murals also show it held slightly above horizontal ⬙ and well below horizontal ⬙ . Later pictures both in China and Korea show a tendency to hold it more upright ⬙ . A Northern Wei sculpture in the Victoria and Albert Museum (6th century) shows a deva with a three-stringed *yuan-xian*, whilst a 5th century Japanese illustration and two 9th century examples in the Shōsōin Treasury have four strings but shorter necks (Shōsōin (*1*) pls.17-19). One has fourteen frets. Five examples occur on Koguryŏ murals and on a Silla pagoda carving.[14] The murals date from the 4th century at Anak (Chang (*1*) pl.13), the late 5th century no.1 tomb at Chang Chuan, the 5th-6th century Three Chambers tomb at Tonggou (Chang (*1*) pl.12), and a 6th century tomb at Tonggou (Yang (*1*) pl. 55). Of the two examples in the front chamber of the Chang Chuan tomb one is a five-stringed instrument with a large peg-box, the other has four strings (fig.25). The example from the Three Chambers tomb is very similar to that in a Wei dynasty painting at Maijishan (fig.26). In each case the deva inclines her head and body to the left over the neck of the instrument, but whereas the Chinese has both knees bent under her in a familiar flying posture the Korean has already adopted the significant Buddhist posture of the right knee bent and the left leg pendant. The Maijishan instrument has a slender neck and its tuning pegs are not visible. Both the Tonggou and the Victoria and Albert Museum examples have broader necks terminating in distinctive peg-boxes, and the pegs of the latter are rounded and prominent.

(A) Tomb of the Three Chambers, Tonggou

(B) Maijishan, Gansu Pr.

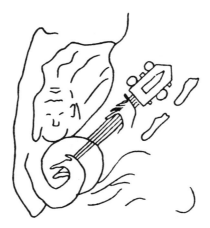

(C) Victoria & Albert Museum

Fig. 26 Three illustrations of devas playing the *yuanxian*

2. The *kŏmun'go*. The earlier of the two famous Korean zithers is said to have been invented in Koguryŏ following the receipt at the court of King Changsu (413-491) of a Chinese *guqin* from the court of the Eastern Jin dynasty.[15] It may not have begun life with the six strings that it later boasted. In the Tomb of the Dancers at Tonggou (5th-6th century), where it is played by two devas, it can clearly be seen to have four strings stretched across fixed frets and to be plucked with a plectrum (fig.27). An openwork metal canopy originally from Horyuji Temple, thought to be the work of a Koguryŏ craftsman, also shows a zither with four strings and fixed frets (fig.28). The instrument played in the *genre* scene in Chang Chuan no.1 tomb is reported to have four pegs.[16] In view of the number of strings, the frets, and the use of the plectrum, it seems possible that either the *yuanxian* or the *pipa* was the source of inspiration for the modifications made to the imported Chinese zither. The illustration of two zithers in tombs of the early and mid-fourth century at T'aesŏngni no.1 and Anak no.3 raises doubts about the date on which the first *guqin* is said to have been received from the Chinese court. However, since both of these zithers are reported to have six strings, it is possible that these are not pictures of the *kŏmun'go* but of the 6-stringed *kum* (see below, p.238), which may have pre-dated the invention of the *kŏmun'go*. This instrument may have been the inspiration for the eventual increase in the number of *kŏmun'go* strings from four to six. In 1957 Hayashi Kenzo advanced the theory that the *kŏmun'go* was none other than the horizontal harp, Ch. *wo konghou,* known from literary sources to have existed in Western Han China (Yang (1) p.128). Lee Hye-Ku disputes this view ((1) pp.419-421) but has not entirely dispelled the possibility of a link between Korean zithers and the earliest *konghou*. Tong Kin-woon describes the latter as "a Chinese instrument...with six strings and fixed frets" (Cao (1) p.11 fn.1). Its appearance is unknown, although the fact that the great Ming dynasty musicologist Prince Zhu Zaiyu surmised a common origin for the *konghou, zheng* and *se* suggests

Fig. 27 Devas playing the *kŏmun'go*

Fig. 28 Musician playing a *kŏmun'go*. Late 6th – early 7th century

that it was believed to be closer to the zithers in form than to the vertical harp. If so, it could have been the model either for the six-stringed zither seen in T'aesŏngni no.1 tomb (which appears to have no frets) or the *kŏmun'go* seen in the Tomb of the Dancers (which has frets but only four strings). The list of Koguryŏ instruments recorded in the *Sui shu* could then begin as follows: *danzheng/kŏmun'go, wo konghou/6-stringed zither, shu konghou/vertical harp*. The term *juzheng* added to the list in the *Samguk sagi* still remains to be interpreted: It may be noted that Korea already had a 5-stringed zither (see page 241) which may have had some earlier relationship with the *zheng* family.

3. The *so* (Ch. [*fei*] *xiao*) panpipes. In China the panpipes are often seen in the hands of musicians both human and divine from the Warring States period onwards. More than forty types have been identified, usually made of bamboo but occasionally of jade, and with pipes ranging in number from ten to twenty four. They are the commonest instrument pictured in murals of the Northern Dynasties, and during the

(A) Nanwuyang, Shandong Province

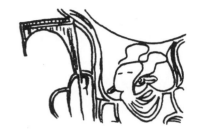

(B) Chongqing

(C) Five Tombs no.4 tomb

(D) Tomb of the Dancers, Tonggou

(E) Cave 249, Dunhuang

(F) Dunhuang

Fig. 29 The panpipes in early Chinese and Korean illustration

first millenium A.D. their shape varies from that of a rectangle with equal length pipes, in which the resonating capacity of each was determined by a deposit of bees-wax in the bottom, to a right-angled triangle ('single wing') or a symmetrical curve similar to the form in which they exist today ('double wing'). It was during the Yuan dynasty that the pipes first assumed their present day black wooden casing decorated with phoenixes (Chuang (1)). In contrast with China they are scarcely ever illustrated in Korea, although the *Sui shu* does include them among the instruments of Koguryŏ, and three examples appear on Koguryŏ tomb murals. Two of these are in the 4th century tomb of Dong Shou at Anak and the third in a 6th century tomb at Tonggou, where the player is a deva. The processional instrument at Anak is roughly symmetrical in form, whilst that from Tonggou is in the commonest early form of a right-angled triangle (fig.29). Panpipes were sent from China to Korea in 1114, 1116 and 1406, but all examples known to the court were said to have been destroyed in the Hideyoshi wars (Song B.S.(2) p.149).

4. The *kak* (Ch. *jue*). The long curved horn and a shorter version of it feature prominently on Koguryŏ murals, though the literary records remain surprisingly silent about them. Four devas play them in the Tomb of the Dancers (plate 73). All four are strange, bi-sexual creatures, not yet freed by their painter's skill to fly above the earth with complete confidence. Their dress, like that of the totally earthbound *kŏmun'go* players, is characterised by slit sleeves and trouser legs and has not yet developed the soft folds and flowing, wind-swept lines of the truly airborne deva. The surviving details of the deva in the late 6th century Chang Chuan no.1 tomb, playing a shorter horn, suggest only slightly more mobility (fig.25, bottom). The *jue* and its relative the *jia* first appeared in China in the Qin and early Han periods. Comparison of Chinese and Korean examples shows variation in the formation of the bell, the length of uncurved pipe and its situation in relation to the curve, the angle of curve, and the way in which the player holds the instrument (fig.30).

5. The *chŏ* (Ch. *[heng] di*). The horizontal flute may have been introduced to China from the Western Regions in the 1st century B.C. It quickly became prominent in banquet, entertainment and military music and must have arrived in Korea during the period of Han colonisation. Compared with a surviving example of the early Korean *taegŭm* family (fig.31) the flutes played by the devas in fig.32 are both longer and more slender. A similar instrument to these is seen in the hands of a Northern Wei deva in cave 283 at Dunhuang (Chang & Li (1)). Devas on bells, pagodas and stupas of the Silla period attest that the general appearance of flutes was not unlike that of Chinese flutes. Specific dimensions were not fixed in China, and it is unlikely that they would have been fixed in Korea.

6. The *changgo*. Another introduction from central Asia, the double-headed hourglass drum, was first used in China in the second century B.C.,[17] and appears in an early Korean illustration in a 6th century tomb at Jian.[18] In Tang murals it is used both as a

(A) Dahuting, Henan Pr.

(B) Anak no.3 tomb

(C) Dengxian, Henan Pr.

(D) Tomb of the Spirits, Lungkang

(E) Tomb of the Three Chambers, Tonggou

(F) Tomb of the Dancers

Fig. 30 The long horn in early Chinese and Korean illustration

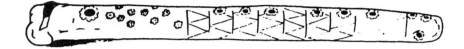

Fig. 31 Pottery flute, 8th - 9th century. Length 40 cms

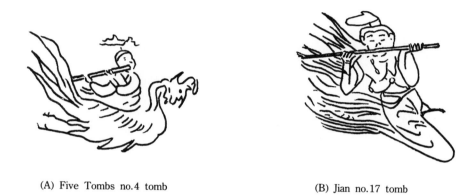

(A) Five Tombs no.4 tomb   (B) Jian no.17 tomb

Fig. 32 Koguryŏ devas playing the horizontal flute

portable waist-drum, slung on a strap across the shoulder, and as an ensemble instrument resting on the knees or on the ground (Zhongguo (1) p.17). Both types were usually more slender in proportion than the 19th and 20th century *changgo* and, especially for popular use, were often made of pottery. Two such examples have survived in Korea from the Koryŏ period, one of celadon[19] and one of *punch'ŏng* ware (plate 18), and a 16th century *punch'ŏng* drum belongs to the Pusan City Museum. This is the drum most commonly used by Korean devas from Silla times until the 20th century, as well as by folk and court musicians, and the *changgo* seen in Buddhist pictures of all kinds repay close study for developments in their shape, stringing and decoration over the centuries.

(ii) *Silla and Koryŏ stone sculptures and bronze bells.*

During the Silla and Koryŏ dynasties series of heavenly musicians were carved on the side panels of square or octagonal pagodas and stupas, and less prominently among the swirling cloud decorations under the eaves separating one storey from the next. Flying devas also appear on decorated end roof tiles (Chang (1) pl.26), and the National Museum at Kyŏngju preserves a fine Silla wall tile from Pulguksa decorated with a musical scene which shows a *pip'a* player. Weathering has adversely affected almost all of these sculptures. Without rubbings, few are as easy to interpret as the set of four shown in plate 76, and none are as perfectly preserved as those on a Chinese carving of 539 A.D. (Yang (*1*) pl.62) or the unique set of twenty four Five Dynasties musicians from the tomb of Wang Jian (*ibid*. pls.80-103), both in Sichuan Province.

The decoration of bronze bells represents one of the peaks of Silla craftsmanship. The great bells of the 8th century formed part of the 'international' phase of Buddhism which prompted the sponsorship of enormous works of art in China and elsewhere. The design of Korean temple bells included three features which distinguished them from Chinese bells, the elaborate suspension knob on top, the panels of nine studs near the top edge, and the pairs of flying devas on opposite sides of the body. Not infrequently these devas were musicians, as were some of those to be found on the ornamental bands around the top and bottom edges of the bell and around the outside of the stud panels. The best examples of this are on the Sangwǒnsa bell (plates 80, 81 and Chang (*1*) pls.22, 23), and the example preserved at the National Museum, Kongju is also a fine one (plate 82).[20] Until the 9th century the devas flew with their knees bent under them; thereafter they also flew cross-legged on a seat of clouds. Both stone and metal craftsmen were expert at carving the swirling draperies of dress, ribbons and clouds and the detail of instruments, and at suggesting the swaying movement of the fairy-like creatures entranced by their own music. The flautist in plate 85 ranks among the greatest examples of musical statuary in the history of world art. In the Koryǒ period, however, the stone figures become heavier, the devas on bronzes smaller, and the artistic effect of pagodas and bells less exciting, and in the outstanding sphere of creative imagination of this era - porcelain decoration - neither deva nor human musicians find any place at all.

One of the most attractive instruments used by the devas on stone sculptures and bells is the harp. Both a horizontal and a vertical harp (Kor. *wagonghu, sugonghu*) are referred to in the Chinese lists of Kǒguryǒ instruments. The former may be of central Asian or western Chinese origin and was known in the Western Han period, although it is not illustrated on any contemporary carved stone. Hayashi Kenzo ((*1*) pp.196-205) believes that the term *wagonghu* refers to the *kǒmun'go,* a view that has not been universally accepted by Chinese or Korean musicologists (see above, p.224). An entertainment scene on an Eastern Han tomb mural shows a player whose left hand appears to be holding the top of an arch (fig.33). The vertical harp was not known in China before the 2nd century A.D. (Yang (*1*) p.128), but

Fig. 33

a song which is apparently of Korean origin, (Ch.) *Konghou yin,* is mentioned among lists of Han dynasty *yue fu.* The implication may be either that *konghou* refers in this context to a board zither or an arched harp already introduced to Korea from China, or that the Koreans were using a different, possibly vertical harp, before it reached China. Neither of these hypotheses would conflict with the interpretation of the passage on Koguryŏ instruments proposed above (p. 225), namely that *wagonghu* refers to the *kŏmun'go* and *sugonghu* to a true harp. Korean tombs, like those in China, have so far failed to reveal any clear artistic evidence on this question. The Shōsōin Treasury possesses the remains of two harps believed to be from Paekche (Shōsōin *(1)* pls.6, 108 – 9). They appear to be identical with the vertical, portable instrument much loved at the Tang court and pictured on the Sangwŏnsa bell. It is also seen on a number of Silla sculptured tiles and the pedestal of a stone pagoda at Chinjŏnsa, held equally across the left and right sides of the body. From the Koryŏ period an example is found on the pagoda now at the National Kyŏngbok University (plate 79), but it is no longer held in the comfortable position adopted by Silla devas, and seems to be more reminiscent of a vertical standing harp than of the lighter, portable instrument. Four harps were included in the Chinese musical gifts of 1114, but they were not *aak* instruments and Korean interest in them, never as strong as the Chinese, seems to disappear during the Koryŏ period. No harps are illustrated in *Akhak kwebŏm,* nor do they appear in any of the *ŭigwe* pictures or in the hands of any Chosŏn dynasty devas. The modern harp now preserved at the National Classical Music Institute in Seoul is clearly related to the later arched harps of south east Asia (Lee H.K. (2) p.68; Williamson (1)) and may or may not be of Chinese ancestry.

(iii) *Chosŏn dynasty paintings.*

Colourfulness and cheerfulness, rather than lightness and other-worldliness, characterise most of the devas of the late Chosŏn dynasty. Some, such as those in the main hall at Pŏpchusa, do have a willowy, wispy quality about them. Most, however, as at Kapsa, are strong and bold, reminiscent of the physical appearance of their predecessors on Wei, Sui and early Tang murals, although Korean ideas of neo-Confucian morality naturally eschewed the semi-nakedness of those early ancestors. Some are dancers, some are dressed in shaman costume; some bear gifts of fruit, but the majority either carry or play musical instruments. Sometimes these have been distorted by the fanciful imagination of the folk artists who painted them, and for whom accuracy was less important than emotional appeal or the need to fit them in to awkwardly shaped spaces created by the position of roof timbers. Comparatively modern additions to the range of flutes, oboes, lutes, cymbals, drums and clappers played by Silla and Koryŏ devas include the *haegŭm,*[21] the *nabal* and the *ulla.* A favourite instrument from the Silla onwards is the *saenghwang.* On some temple paintings it has an exaggerated, curved mouthpiece, and on some the shorter mouthpiece of today. The latter is more akin to that of the Han dynasty (fig.34), though the windchest to which it is now fixed is much larger than it was then. The overall length

(A) Han dynasty brick

(B) Dunhuang

(C) Pŏmŏsa, Pusan

(D) Pŏmŏsa, Pusan

(E) Pŏpchusa

(F) Pang'wŏnsa

Fig. 34 The *saenghwang* in Chinese and Korean illustration

of the pipes varies in Korean illustrations, as it does on Dunhuang murals (Zhongguo *(1)* pp.5-6), but no illustrations are capable of indicating the occasional variation in the number of pipes. Diagrams in *Akhak kwebŏm* show thirteen and seventeen and the text refers to versions with nineteen and thirty six, although the latter was only experimental during the reign of King Sejong. Some unfamiliarity with the shape of the *saenghwang* on the part of the monk-artists living in the countryside in the 18th or 19th century might be excused on the grounds that the instrument had so lapsed into disuse following the devastation of the Hideyoshi and Manchu invasions that it had had to be officially re-introduced from China and re-constructed in the second half of the 17th century (Song B.S.(2) pp.148-151).

2) ATTENDANTS ON BUDDHA IN PARADISE

PLATE 95 Attendants on Amitabha Buddha in the Pure Land Paradise. 1323 A.D. 204.2×139.1cms. Chionin Temple, Kyoto, Japan. Groups of musicians and dancers may be seen in the buildings on the left and right sides of the picture. Their instruments include the *taegŭm,* bent-necked *pip'a, saenghwang,* and *changgo.*

PLATE 96 Female musicians among attendants on Buddha. Late 18th century. Azure Cloud Hall, T'ongdosa. Their instruments include the conch shell, *pip'a, changgo, taegŭm,* cymbals, and *puk* drum.

3) GUARDIAN KINGS

PLATE 97 Guardian King holding a *pip'a,* incised on the back of a portable Buddhist shrine of gilt-bronze. 11th-12th century. H.28 cms. *National Museum, Seoul*

PLATE 98 Guardian King holding a *pip'a.* Sculpture from the gateway of T'ongdosa. 18th century. Height 3.05 m

PLATE 99 Guardian King holding a *pip'a.* Panel from behind the main altar in the Hall of Supreme Delight, Sŏngnamsa. 20th century. Height c.1.2 m

The four Heavenly Kings (*Sa Ch'ŏnwang*) were not gods but protective and controlling figures who lived at the centre of the universe on Mount Sumera. As attendants upon Buddha they were associated with the devas. They promised happiness to those who honoured Buddha, the Law and the Priesthood, and they supervised the lowest of the Buddhist series of heavens, where those who were on the path to *Nirvana* but had so far only attained the first of the Ten Main Vows, the promise not to kill, awaited rebirth. They commanded the four elements of fire, air, water and earth.

The Kings were illustrated at Dunhuang and were first given their own halls (Ch. *tian wang dian*) in the Tang dynasty, a promotion from the rather lowly role of gatekeeper which they did not generally attain in Korea, though in temples there they were often portrayed behind the main altar in the Great Buddha Hall. The King of the East (*Chinguk ch'ŏnwang*), or less commonly the King of the South or the King of the North, carries a sword or a four- or five-stringed, bent-necked *pip'a*. Music was thought to give him power over the elements, and there were musicians among the army of spirits under his command. Sometimes his countenance is fierce, sometimes smiling.

The picture on the back of the shrine (plate 97) is one of the earliest showing a king holding the lute. He holds it at an angle of 45° across his chest and plays it with a plectrum. Four tuning pegs are clearly seen, although only three strings are visible. In Chošon dynasty temple gateways the figures of the kings are either modelled in clay, plaster or wood or represented pictorially. A large 19th century banner from a gateway in the Taegu area showing the King of the East with a *pip'a* hangs on the wall of the west staircase in the British Museum.

4) THE IMMORTALS

PLATE 100 attr. Ch'oe Myŏng-nyong (1567-1621), *Immortal musicians and dancers.* 143 × 87.5 cms. *National Museum, Seoul*

PLATE 101 Kim Hong-do, *Immortals.* 21×52.5 cms. *Seoul National University Museum*

PLATE 102 Kim Hong-do, *Immortals.* 28.4 × 41.5cms. *National Museum, Seoul*

PLATE 103 Kim Yang-gi (brush-name Kŏngwŏn, late 18th cent.), *An Immortal playing a saenghwang.* 107.5 × 70cms. *National Museum, Seoul*

The Immortals were human beings who by dint of extraordinary mental or physical behaviour had achieved a metamorphosis at the instant of their mortal death, and then continued to roam the universe in physical form but with divine powers. Like Bodhisattvas they appeared before favoured humans to offer advice and blessings. Usually they were seen only singly, though Chinese believers, with their love of numerical associations, often grouped them into bands of compatible spirits. They were favourite subjects for artists both in China and Korea, where Tanwŏn painted some of the best known of them in the firm, spontaneous brush-style that characterises the best of his *genre* works. Hoam Museum of Fine Art possesses one of the most impressive of these, an eight-panel screen 132.8 cms high that shows his command of space and composition to be as complete when he worked on a large surface as it was when he painted an album leaf or a small fan.[22]

Since the Zhou dynasty Chinese philosophers had identified the connection between the sagely man and music, and had understood the power of music to influence man and his environment. This was not only a Confucian principle. Searching for the laws of relationship and harmony in the universe, Zhuangzi described the music of heaven as bringing order to the four seasons and the ten thousand things, and delighting the mind of the perceptive man with its soundless perfection. In a passage that appears to anticipate a Zen-style paradox but that also expresses a mystical concept of ecstasy, the ultimate in perfect unity between man, spirit and universe that was later echoed by St. John of the Cross,[23] Zhuangzi "puts the performance of music on a cosmic scale and portrays it as an event in nature, in contrast to the Confucian view,...in which it is an event in society"(DeWoskin (1) p.62):

> Then I played it [said the Yellow Emperor] with unwearying notes and tuned it to the common of spontenaity. Therefore there seemed to be a chaos where things grew in thickets together, a maturity where nothing takes form, a universal plucking where nothing gets pulled, a clouded obscurity in which there is no sound. It moved in no direction at all, rested in mysterious shadow. Some called it death, some called it life, some called it fruit, some called it flower. It flowed and scattered, and bowed before no constant tone. The world, perplexed by it, went to the sage for instruction, for the sage is the comprehender of true form and the completer of fate. When the heavenly mechanism is not put into action and yet the five vital organs are all complete - this may be called the music of heaven. Wordless, it delights the mind. Therefore the Lord of Yang sang its praises thus : 'Listen - you do not hear its sound ; look - you not see its form. It fills all heaven and earth, enwraps all the six directions.'[24]

Such perfection naturally surpassed any artistic representation, but allusions to it are to be found in east Asian landscape painting, which on the one hand reduced man to his proper perspective in comparison with the forces of nature and creation, and on the other put into his hands, or those of his servant, the means - the musical instrument - whereby he could control and achieve union with the whole universe. Similarly, painters of the Daoist Immortals, by portraying them with a book or musical instrument, bore witness to the deeper truth about the power of these physical objects.

An early example of the magical properties of the *saenghwang* shows a phoenix dancing to its music (fig.35). The player is Wang Ziqiao, and some illustrations of this well known Daoist legend also show the Immortal Fo Qiugong being conjured up by his sublime performance. Such pictures, like the dancing figures in plate 100, demonstrate that ecstasy was not necessarily either a serious or a solitary state.

PLATE 104 Anonymous folk artist, *The God of Longevity*, or *Spirit of the South Pole Star*. Chosŏn dynasty. 98 × 54 cms. *Emille Museum*

Fig. 35 Koryŏ dynasty mirror showing a phoenix dancing to the playing of a *saenghwang*

5. Entertainment Music

PLATE 105 Pottery jar decorated with animal and human figures. 5th-6th century Height 34.2 cms. Diameter at mouth 22.4 cms. *National Museum, Kyŏngju*

PLATE 106 Detail of the above

PLATE 107 Lid of a steamer decorated with figures. Silla period. Diameter 14.8 cms *Ewha Women's University Museum, Seoul*

Credit for the origination of the *sanjo* form, and for streamlining the large and heavy court *kayagŭm* to make it more manageable for an agile, vigorous performance, is usually given to Kim Ch'ang-jo (1865-1920). He is said to have been awoken to the creative possibilities of improvising on folk tunes for his own instrument by the lively style of *sinawi*. The popularity of *sanjo* in modern times, and the fact that improvisation has all but disappeared as it has been reduced to a standardised form and notated for popular use, does not deprive it of some of the dazzling showmanship which once indicated its links with the supernatural world of the shaman. Credit for the invention of the *kayagŭm* itself, far back in the 6th century, goes nominally to King Kasil of Kaya, who is said to have modelled it on the Chinese *zheng* and to have ordered his musician U Rŭk to compose music for it.[25] U Rŭk's twelve pieces appear to have been based on Kaya folk melodies, thus explaining, probably, the dislike of the Silla musicians Pŏpchi, Kyego and Mandŏk referred to above (p.28) The link between the *kayagŭm* and folk music was therefore established at an early date, even though the main feature of the instrument's known history over the next thirteen hundred years was its use in court music and *chŏngak*. Whether or not King Kasil really did have a hand in the making of the *kayagŭm,* or whether he simply took the credit for the work of U Rŭk and others, can never be known. Indeed, we may wonder what these eminent gentlemen of the court actually did towards the invention of the instrument in question. Consider, for example, the *Samguk sagi*'s implication that when U Rŭk first fled with his *kayagŭm* to Silla he took with him the first and perhaps the only example of a new instrument, one reputed to be of royal manufacture. It is reasonable to assume that King Chinhŭng and his courtiers in Silla would have prized it highly, confining its use at least for a while to music at court. Yet on stylistic and circumstantial evidence the pottery figures shown in these plates, which have no apparent claim to courtly origins, cannot date from much later than 551, and are almost certainly earlier. Two of them show zithers in the hands of women, one of them visibly pregnant, accompanying sexual acts. The women have been identifid as shamans and the occasions as fertility rites.[26] Figures of naked people with prominent sexual organs appear on a number of Silla pottery pieces and among contemporary Japanese wares, and probably depict members of the lower

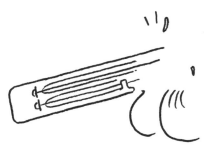

Fig. 36

classes. In other words, a zither was already in use at the lower end of Silla society and doubtless of Kaya society too before U Rŭk's defection in 551. Was it the *kayagŭm* or was it a different kind of zither? The instrument in plate 105 is clearly marked with six incised strings, two more than the *kŏmun'go* of the northern state of Koguryŏ. Moreover, the absence of frets, so plainly visible in the picture of a *kŏmun'go* in figure 28, and the presence of the distinctive ram's horns, which never had any connection with the *kŏmun'go,* rule out the possibility of its being the latter. It must have been another kind of zither. A zither with six strings is depicted on the north wall of the inner chamber at Taesŏngni (fig.36) and the zither accompanying a dancer in the rear chamber of Anak no. 3 tomb is reported to have six strings (fig.42).[27] These instruments have no frets; neither do they have ram's horns, which may thus have been a peculiarity of Silla workmanship. It was presumably this zither, the one referred to in historical texts simply as *kum,* that Paekkyŏl of Silla played in the 5th century (p.88). In other words, there is evidence for the widespread use of a six-stringed instrument long before the middle of the 6th century. We cannot be certain of what King Kasil or his musicians exactly did, but it seems probable that they doubled the number of this zither's strings and added moveable bridges, thereby bringing the Korean instrument into line with the contemporary style of the Chinese *zheng.*

PLATE 108 Horn players on the south wall of the front chamber, Anak no.3 tomb

Among the forms of banqueting entertainment that were accompanied by music in Han China were acrobatics and gymnastics, juggling, dancing, wrestling and animal acts. Even feasts following funeral rites were attended by such jovial performances, so that the scenes shown on tomb murals may sometimes represent the wakes of the deceased person. Murals and the unique pottery model from Jinan (fig.37) show that the ensemble used for these occasions included the mouthorgan, panpipes, horizontal and vertical flutes and a zither, usually the large 23-stringed *se*. Percussion instruments include the uncommon sight of two bells hanging obliquely from a frame and sets of two and four stone chimes (fig.38). Mostly, however, they are drums, either the very large and ornately decorated vertical stand drum, *yinggu,* or smaller horizontal drums. The *yinggu* was a double-headed drum often, but not always, played by two men. The example in fig.37 (top right) has a hole with a raised rim on its upper surface and must once have borne the tall decoration of birds, leaves and canopies that distinguished this fine drum in Warring States and Han times and anticipated the superstructure that surmounted its Korean descendant, the *kŏn'go*. Smaller drums which appear in entertainment ensembles include the hand-held stringed drum (fig.15), the hand- or foot-struck *bofu* (fig.38, front rank of musicians), and on the Jinan model an unusual drum on a short pedestal, mounted facing the player with its head at an angle of 60° to the ground. Ensembles with four or six members are common, but fig.38 shows that elaborate entertainments sometimes called for larger troupes.

Fig. 37 Han dynasty pottery model of an entertainment scene

Fig. 38 Han dynasty decorated brick of an entertainment scene

Fig. 39

Fig. 40 Han dynasty mural of an
entertainment scene

Unfortunately the earliest Koguryŏ tombs lack the sophisticated and detailed forms of decoration that reveal so much about Han music, with the exception perhaps of the processional scene discussed above (p.195). In that same tomb, however, with its memorial to the Chinese official Dong Shou, are two illustrations of entertainment. In the front chamber, immediately to the left of the entrance on the south wall, is a picture of five musicians. Flanking the doorway on the opposite side stand seven men holding banners and ceremonial implements, while on the adjoining east wall are two wrestlers. The musicians are arranged in two groups. In the foreground kneel a drummer, a figure holding a set of panpipes, and one on the right who may be a singer. The type of drum is not clear. It is mounted on a shaft but is not large enough to be a *yinggu*. It appears to be single-headed and its head is approximately at face level with the kneeling player (fig.39). It may be of the same kind as the one seen with a group of musicians in a Han tomb at Dongwa Yazi (fig.40). Some distance behind the trio stand two men playing the long horn, *kak,* which curves away over the right shoulder and opens out into a flared bell. One of the two men is no longer visible and his presence can only be deduced from the bell of his instrument, the position of which suggests that he is facing his companion. With only an occasional exception, the *kak* does not appear in Chinese representations of entertainment music, where indeed it would seem to be out of place under normal circumstances.[28] Nor are banners and ceremonial implements generally seen in entertainment scenes depicted in Han murals. Yet Lee Hye-Ku has argued that the three pictures on the south and east walls form an integral scene and that this is not a continuation of the procession on the wall of the east corridor (Lee H.K.(3)). No Han illustrations of wrestling matches show whether or not they usually took place in the presence of such formal paraphernalia and to the rousing blast of curved horns. If they did, then the excited atmosphere of the occasion and the noise from the spectators might have rendered normal music inappropriate and thus account for the smaller than usual ensemble shown in the Anak picture. The presence of a singer and the panpipes, and the absence of reeds and stringed instruments, may also relate to the special requirements of the situation. Three possible explanations for this series of pictures may be proposed: First, that it represents a rare illustration of a specific type of entertainment music which differed noticeably from that played for acrobatics, games and dances, a form of entertainment to which, perhaps, Dong Shou was particularly addicted and which may have accompanied his funeral; second, that entertainment music in 4th century Koguryŏ, even when portrayed in the context of a Chinese official's tomb, had undergone changes which rendered it unlike that of the more relaxed and genteel surroundings of the Han court; and third, that the four groups of people in question, horn players, musicians, flag-bearers and wrestlers, do not in fact constitute a single picture, but refer separately to incidents or interests in Dong Shou's life. There are, after all, some five metres and a wide doorway between the musical picture and that of the wrestlers.

PLATE 109 Lady with a servant carring a zither. Detail of a mural on the south wall of the front chamber, no. 1 tomb, Chang Chuan, Jilin province, China. Late 5th century.

From her dress and demeanour the subject of this plate appears to be a lady of some distinction, possibly the wife of the nobleman buried in the tomb, possibly a singer. The servant girl walking behind her carries an instrument which seems to be a five-stringed zither with tuning pegs. Chu Chae-gŏl *(1)* calls it an *ohyŏn* (not to be confused with the *ohyŏn* lute). Both the *Sui shu* and the *Samguk sagi* refer to an instrument of this name in their descriptions of the Koyuryŏ band. The fact that they list it after the *pip'a* and not among the zithers implies that their compilers identified the name with the Chinese *wuxian* lute, known in Korea as the *hyangpip'a*. This could have been due to confusion on their part, the *ohyŏn* zither having disappeared in the meantime. The suggestion is made above (p.65) that the five-stringed zither may have been a Korean survival of the Chinese *zhu*. No illustration of this instrument earlier than the 13th century (in Chen Yang's *Yue shu*) is known, so its original appearance cannot be confirmed. Until further relevant evidence comes to light the positive identification of this zither must remain, like the silver pieces from King Munyong's tomb, problematic.

Fig. 41 Detail from plate 109

PLATE 110 Dancer from a mural in the rear chamber, no.3 tomb, Anak. 357 A.D.

PLATE 111 Zither player and dancer. Detail from a mural in no.1 tomb, Chang Chuan, Jilin Province. Late 5th century

PLATE 112 Detail from a mural in the Tomb of the Dancers, Tonggou, Liaoning Province, China. 6th century

Dancers appear frequently in the company of musicians on Han tomb murals and it comes as no surprise to find them on the walls of Koguryŏ tombs. In China they might be accompanied by flutes, reeds, zithers and drums.[29] In Koguryŏ we find a trio consisting of zither, *wanham* and long vertical flute (*changjŏk*) on the east wall of the rear chamber of Dong Shou's tomb (fig.42), an almost identical combination to that seen on a Han dynasty wall painting from Bang Taizi, Liaoning Province, of zither, *qiangdi* and *pipa* (fig.43) The dress of the dancer at Anak, as well as his physiognomy and complexion, show him to be of central Asian rather than east Asian race. His presence on the wall of a Chinese official's tomb in northern Korea coincides with a time when musical instruments from central Asia are thought to have been arriving in the Far East. The ensemble which accompanied dancers could be reduced to a minimum of a zither and a singer, or to a zither alone. An example of the latter occurs in no. 1 tomb at Chang Chuan (plate 111), and corresponds almost exactly to the figures from a Han entertainment scene in fig.44.

Fig. 42 Dancer in the rear chamber, Anak no. 3 tomb

Fig. 43 Han musical ensemble, Bang Taizi, Liaoning

Fig. 44 Han dynasty dancer with zither accompaniment

Although male musicians are in the majority amongst the performers seen in Chinese tomb illustrations, female players do also occur and dancers are both male and female in roughly equal proportions. The principal feature of female dancers' dress, standard from the Warring States period in China to modern times in Korea, is the long, brightly coloured sleeves that hang down below the wrists (plate 5). Sleeves assist in identifying dancers in the Chang Chuan *genre* mural; and nearly fifteen hundred years later they are still adding to the sumptuary splendour of court banquets (plates 29-32). The performance by dancers and singers in plate 112 closely resembles a fragmentary scene on the south wall of the front chamber at Chang Chuan (fig.45).

Fig. 45 Chorus and dancers, Chang Chuan no. 1 tomb

PLATE 113 Kim Chung-gun (brush-name Kisan, late 19th century), *A komun'go player.* 22.5×18.5 cms. *Korean Christian Museum, Sungjon University, Seoul*

Akhak kwebŏm, in common with Chinese musical encyclopoedias and *guqin* manuals, states that the zither is played with the right hand. The great majority of pictures do indeed show stringed instruments of all kinds played thus. In this plate, however, as in fig.28, the *kŏmun'go* is laid to the right of the performer's knees. The right hand is being used to depress the strings and it is the left hand that holds the *sultae*. Examples of Chinese zithers played in a left-handed position are not infrequently seen in Han and Nanbei zhao tomb decorations (for example, in fig.44). A left-handed *pipa* player is occasionally seen, as in cave 379 at Dunhuang (Sui dynasty., cf. plate 122), and the horizontal flute is quite commonly played with the mouth at the right hand end rather than the left, which is the normal playing position today. In the *Chinch'an ŭigwe* screen of 1902 (plates 29,30) the *taegŭm* players in the left half of the terrace orchestra hold their instruments to the right, while those in the right half hold theirs' to the left. Too many examples of these 'unorthodox' playing positions exist for them all to be dismissed as errors on the part of ignorant artists. Pictorial evidence from central Asia, China and Korea suggests that in former times players of many instruments were less rigid about the position in which they held their instruments than their successors are today.

* * * * *

Between the two extremes of literati and folk painting comes the class known as *genre* painting. It is the artistic equivalent of *hyangak,* and just as Korea's most distinguished compositions fall within that category, so do *genre* paintings stand out as her most spontaneous and characteristic works of art. They are not uniquely Korean, though Korean artists were outstandingly proficient at painting them. In China, for example, the paintings of Wu Wei (1459-1508) had already anticipated both the style and content of Tanwŏn's *genre* works (fig.46). Neither are they numerous, even in the 18th century when the inspiration to paint in this fashion was at its height, but they date from as far back as the wall paintings of the 5th century and they include many illustrations of music and dance. These are the pictures that show the Korean people in relaxed mood, enjoying their music without taking it too seriously, portraying their emotions and behaviour with the simple, deft touch of the cartoonist just as plainly as the landscapist conveys the atmosphere of mountain and river scenery. The situations they describe, though often in settings unfamiliar to our contemporary social experience in the West, can still evoke our empathy, and sparing though they may be in line and detail they convey a convincing sense of reality.

PLATE 114 Sin Yun-bok, *Girl stringing a kŏmun'go.* 27.4 × 21.5 cms. *National Museum, Seoul*

PLATE 115 Sin Yun-bok, *Picnic by a lotus pond.* 28.3 × 35.2 cms. *Kansong Museum of Fine Arts, Seoul*

Fig. 46 Wu Wei, *Strolling entertainers* (detail)

PLATE 116 Sin Yun-bok, *Kisaeng with a saenghwang*. Album leaf. 28.3 × 35.2 cms. *Kansong Museum of Fine Arts, Seoul*

PLATE 117 Sin Yun-bok, *Kisaeng by a lotus pond*. 29.6 × 24.8 cms. *National Museum, Seoul*

Hyewŏn was a military official, a member of the Academy, and one of the outstanding painters in the *genre* form. He had a penchant for *kisaeng* and the slightly erotic treatment of some of his subjects, a tendency that was not unfamiliar in China but that may have been responsible for the loss of his Academy membership at the more straight-laced Korean court. Many *kisaeng* were accomplished musicians, and music features prominently in Hyewŏn's work. Plate 114 is a finely detailed study of a girl tuning her *kŏmun'go,* stretching the strings with her left hand while with her right she turns the pegs under the string-holder. She wears the typical costume and piled-up hairstyle of the 18th century courtesan, as many of Hyewŏn's subjects do. In plate 115 music is stimulating an affectionate mood in the *kisaeng*'s admirers. It comes from a court *kayagŭm,* not an instrument that some scholars would wish to see represented in such a provocative scene, but this was a time when critics such as Hyewŏn were challenging or poking fun at the social and cultural values of the *yangban* class, and the duties of *kisaeng* made an entertaining target.

PLATE 118 Anon., *Picnic in the back garden*. 18th century. 52.8 × 33.1 cms. *National Museum, Seoul*

PLATE 119 Yi Kyŏng-yun (brush-name Nakp'a, 1545- ?), *Looking at the moon*. Album leaf. 31.2 × 24.9 cms. *Korea University Museum*

PLATE 120 Yi Pang-un (18th-19th century), *Playing the zither under a pine tree*. 109 × 59 cms. *National Museum, Seoul*

PLATE 121 Kim Hong-do, *Tanwŏn Pavilion*. 135 × 78.5 cms. *National Museum, Seoul*

When Korean scholar artists painted in their more obviously Chinese style, and especially when they painted landscapes, music tended to occur in the same cliché situations as it often did in Chinese art, associated with water, moonlight, solitude, friendship, and intimations of venerability such as gnarled rocks and pine trees. In Korean art, just as in Chinese, the servant is often to be seen following in his master's footsteps and carrying his zither to a mountain retreat. The educated Korean picture-lover was well aware of the philosophical messages conveyed to him by such scenes, but if the purpose of the picture was to provide intellectual stimulus, its delight couched in the compatibility of the 'three eternities' - painting, poetry and calligraphy – as much as in the choice and execution of its subject, then we may ask whether it mattered, any more than it did in religious art, whether it was accurate or not as a representation of Korean reality. The Chinese artist might spurn the painstaking copying of the panorama in favour of the spirit that breathed through the eidetic image. The Korean artist, too, painting a delightfully realistic picture in a Chinese style, had perhaps less reason to be concerned about the accuracy of his subject matter than the *genre* painter.[30] So do the musical examples in Korean literati art represent Korean musical practice, or do they simply reflect musical clichés borrowed from their Chinese colleagues? The answer may be 'yes' to each alternative. It is entirely probable that people in Korea should have derived pleasure from music in a riverine or moonlit setting, either singly or in company, just as over the centuries countless Korean servants must have plodded along paths bearing their masters' zithers. The Korean scholar enjoyed playing both the *kŏmun'go* and the *pip'a* as solo instruments and also became fond of the *kayagŭm* as the *sanjo* form developed in the 19th century. The *kŏmun'go* in particular was a symbol of his genteel social outlook, although the intellectual and philosophical pretensions he claimed with it, strongly as they were expressed as a Korean response to the deeply rooted lore of the *guqin* in China, lacked the latter's conviction of originality and already had an outmoded air about them as new, native musical forms took shape. It was the *kayagŭm* that led the way in solo instrumental development in the 19th century, and insofar as it was the *kayagŭm* of the folk tradition that was used for *sanjo*, it is fitting for this instrument to be pictured in rural settings. The proper place for the *kŏmun'go*, traditionally associated with a man's scholarly satisfaction, was in the study, yet it does not appear in early examples of the category of folk art known as *ch'aekkŏri* ('book pile scenery'), in which the essential items in the study appeared to be paper, brushes, inkstick and inkstone. Only in later times, when *sanjo* had established itself, were the constituents of *ch'aekkŏri* increased to include the *kayagŭm*, flowers and food.

PLATE 122 Grey pottery steamer surmounted by a figure playing a lute. Kaya period (5th–early 6th century A.D.). Height c.21 cms. Diameter c.16 cms. *Tong'a University Museum, Pusan*

PLATE 123 Grey pottery figure of a person playing a lute. 5th–6th century. Height 12 cms. *National Museum, Kyŏngju*

Two versions of the pear-shaped lute with integral neck and body were known in the Far East, one with four strings and one with five. The former originated in western central Asia and reached China during the Han dynasty. An early illustration of it may be seen in a tomb painting from Liaoyang, Liaoning Province (fig.43). It had a shortish, bent neck and four frets, and was normally played by plucking the strings with a plectrum, although from the 7th century onwards the fingers were also sometimes used. Its Chinese name is said to have been derived from the strokes, downwards (*pi*) and upwards (*pa*), with which it was played by musicians on horseback beyond the frontiers of China.

Fig. 47 The *wuxian*

The five-stringed lute, known in China as the *wuxian* ('five strings'), probably came from India and arrived in north China about the 5th century A.D. It was longer and more slender than the *pipa,* had a straight neck and five frets, and was also played with a plectrum (fig.47). Of the two types, the *pipa* appears more frequently in Chinese wall paintings, at Dunhuang for example. Five fine examples of the four-stringed lute and one of the five-stringed version, all probably of the 8th century, are preserved in the Shōsōin Treasury at Nara (Shōsōin *(1)* pls.7-16, 112-123). Pictorial evidence shows that both lutes were generally held with the bowl against the player's stomach and the neck pointing to the side, either horizontally or towards the ground at an angle of 45° (Zhongguo *(1)* pp.14-15). Less commonly the neck was raised above the horizontal to an angle of approximately 30° and occasionally it is shown in a more upright position still (Shōsōin *(1)* pl.196).

It is not known when either of the two lutes first appeared in Korea. In view of the earlier presence of the *pipa* in the north-east of China it would be surprising if it were not the first to have been heard in the three kingdoms, and the proportions of the instruments held by the figures in these plates clearly suggest that they are *pipas.* The *Sui shu* lists both among the instruments played by the Koguryŏ orchestra at the Chinese court in the early 7th century. The *Samguk sagi* says that the five-stringed lute, known in Korea as the *hyangpip'a* ('native *pip'a*'), originated in Silla of an unknown maker, but this is clearly erroneous and may indicate that the name *hyangpip'a* was coined during the Silla period to distinguish it from the four-stringed version, more popular in China and referred to subsequently but misleadingly in Korea as the *tangpip'a.* To judge from the frequency of illustration in the Silla and Koryŏ periods, it was this instrument that was also the more commonly used in Korea. By the 15th century it was said that "any of the ordinary people who learn music always begin with the [four-stringed] *pip'a*", whereas the *hyangpip'a* is recorded as being too difficult for most people to master (Chang *(1)* p.92 n.155). Both instruments were photographed in the hands of musicians at the Government Music Department by Andreas Eckardt around 1930 (*(1)* pl.25), but their total disappearance in performance since then is hard to explain.

The *Akhak kwebŏm* shows that the *tangpip'a* had twelve frets and the *hyangpip'a* ten, although examples now preserved at the National Classical Music Institute have ten and twelve respectively. The *hyangpip'a* was played with a short stick. In earlier dynasties the angle at which the instrument was held appears to have been the same as in China, but by the 18th century a more upright position was favoured. A relative of the *pip'a*, the moon-shaped *wŏlgŭm*, had long been played in this way.

PLATE 124 Yi Kyŏng-yun, *Playing the pip'a in a boat.* 44.3 × 23.8 cms. *Seoul National University Museum*

PLATE 125 Kim Hong-do, *Scholar playing the pip'a.* 27.9 × 37 cms. *National Museum, Seoul*

In the first half of the Chosŏn dynasty painting still exhibited the strong, formal style of the Chinese Northern Song Academy. Hyŏndongja (below, plate 138) demonstrates this, his landscapes recalling the majesty of Guo Xi's cliffs and waterfalls. So does Nakp'a, a member of the royal family whose work included landscapes, figures and animals, although the emotional subject of plate 119, redolent of loneliness and homesickness, softens its effect. By the 18th century paintings still depicted the upper class enjoying cultural pursuits in rather stylised, quasi-Chinese situations (plate 121). The *genre* painters of the era, however, surpassed such conventions and began to reveal the intimate lives of both upper and lower classes in a way that was both novel and daring in Korea. Tanwŏn was outstanding as a painter of landscapes, portraits, religious scenes, and especially *genre* subjects. His greatness is attributed on the one hand to his all-round versatility – he excelled in painting Confucian, Buddhist and Daoist themes, large-scale murals, impressionistic album sketches, detailed scrolls and screens and delicate miniature fans – and on the other to his excellent sense of composition and simplicity of brushwork. He is best known today for *genre* paintings that are unpretentious in character and execution yet evocative and entertaining as a description of traditional Korean life. Usually, like the album of village scenes from which plate 129 is taken, they are smaller pictures. Renowned as something of a rebel, Tanwŏn more frequently chose his subjects from the daily life of the common people than Hyewŏn did, and as plate 125 shows, when he did paint the literati he dared to do so tongue-in-cheek.

PLATE 126 Stoneware figure of a flute player. 5th-6th century. Height 28.3 cms. *Avery Brundage Museum, California*

No vertical flute used in Korea today has the proportions of those shown in the early art of the peninsula. The type illustrated in the rear chamber of Dong Shou's tomb at Anak, the so-called 'long flute', *changjŏk*, stretched from the mouth of the kneeling player to the ground, probably in excess of 70 cms. It was a Chinese instrument, seen in figs. 43 and 48, but evidence for its presence in Korea is scanty and it does not seem to have been widely used there (Lee H.K.(3) p.13). The lengths of the three notched flutes described in *Akhak kwebŏm* are c.65 cms (the *chŏk*), c.60 cms (the *t'ongso*), and c.57 cms (the *yak*). The instrument shown in this plate, which also appears to be a notched flute, may be estimated as approximately 45 cms in length. Its circumference is greater than any known Korean flute today, closer perhaps to that of the *shakuhachi*. Its appearance suggests that it was made of either bamboo or pottery. In China the word *xiao* was used for both a single vertical pipe and for a multiple set banded together to form the panpipes. When, therefore, the *Sui shu* and the *Samguk sagi* list the *xiao/so* among the instruments of Koguryŏ they could be referring to the flute seen here as well as to the panpipes discussed above. No other term appears in their lists which might indicate the vertical flute.

Fig. 48 The long flute (Ch. *qiangdi*) in a Han dynasty ensemble

PLATE 127 Chin Che-hai (1691-1769), *Playing a flute in the moonlight*. 100 × 56.7 cms. *Seoul National University Museum*

PLATE 128 Kim Ung-an (18th century), *Listening to a flute on the river bank*. 20.6 × 37.2 cms. *National Museum, Seoul*

PLATE 129 Kim Hong-do, *Dancing boy*. Album leaf. 24 × 28 cms. *National Museum, Seoul*

Plate 129 is one of Tanwŏn's best known paintings, and commentators have consistently and properly referred to its sense of uninhibited gaiety and enthusiastic movement. The six *kwangdae* musicians accompanying the dancer constitute a *samhyŏn yukkak* ensemble, literally 'three strings and six horns'. The original meaning of this term is now lost, although the fact that the name *Samhyŏn yŏngsan hoesang* is given to the wind version of the suite may imply that it referred to a group of wind instruments. The present day ensemble consists of two *p'iri, taegŭm, haegŭm* (counted as a wind instrument because of its ability to play sustained notes), *changgo* and *puk*, identical to Tanwŏn's band except for the use of the *puk* in place of the *chwago*. It is the same group that plays for the sword dance in plate 135 and for the more formal entertainment in plate 35. *Dancing boy* is unusual for showing the front view of the players: Most groups of instrumentalists, as will be seen from the plates in this book, had to be content with the sight of their own backs. They were rarely the subjects of a picture, and were usually of little interest compared with the nobility whose entertainment they helped to provide.

PLATE 130 Scenes from daily life: Detail from the picture in the Great Buddha Hall, Pangwŏnsa, Seoul. 20th century

PLATE 131 Scenes from daily life: Detail from the picture in the Great Buddha Hall, Yŏngjusa, Suwŏn. 18th century

PLATE 132 Anon., *Masked dancers*. 1724 A.D. 74.2 × 43 cms. *Private collection*

PLATE 133 Anon., *P'ansori performance*. Detail from a screen decorated with a view of P'yŏngyang Castle. 19th century. Panels 131 × 39 cms. *Seoul National University Museum*

PLATE 134 Kim Chung-gun, *A p'ansori singer*. 25.5 × 18.5 cms. *Korean Christian Museum, Sungjon University, Seoul*

Kwangdae troupes provided local entertainment as early as the Koryŏ dynasty, when they played *sandae* masked dance dramas and spectacular *narye* plays with acrobatics from China.[31] One of the most popular dances performed by their successors in the Chosŏn dynasty was the *ch'ŏyong* dance, which they sometimes gave to envoys in the hope that the masks would frighten evil spirits away from them on their travels. Impromptu dances around the villages would be less elaborate but just as lively (plate 132).

Fig. 49 Han dynasty decorated
tile of tightrope walkers

Plate 131 shows an acrobatic feat that has been popular in both China and Korea for many centuries and is still accompanied by a farmers' band in Korea today. No

Fig. 50 Tightrope walking, from
the *San cai tu hui*

musicians appear on the Han brick illustration (fig.49) and the man beating the gong in the 17th century picture (fig.50) may be doing so to attract attention, but in 18th century Korea the hypnotic effect of *nongak* may well have been more important. Tightrope walking was more than a simple balancing act, the performer there exhibiting powers that in the shaman would have been attributed to the entry of a spirit into her body (*sinmyŏng*). The tightrope walker, too, could enter a trance state when she would dance, act, and do such unbelievable tricks that the onlookers would be wholly caught up in her escape from reality.[32]

Of all the *kwangdae* skills, the one that was the most highly regarded as a cultural form was the singing of *p'ansori*.

How delightful is the *kwangdae's* way of life,
But how truly difficult!
The first requirement for a *kwangdae* is good looks,
The second is outstanding skill in narration,
And the third musical talent and dramatic ability.
Dramatic ability means to be full of life and grace:
Numerous changes in an instant –
At one minute a fairy, the next a ghost;
He'll make his audience laugh and cry –
The brave as well as the emotional, both men and women, old and young,
Dramatic ability is indeed the most difficult of all.
Musical talent means the ability to distinguish the five tones,
To manipulate the six pitches, and
To sing by means of voice control from the body.
This too is a hard thing to do.
Narrative skill means to tell a story as clearly as fine gold and beautiful jade,
To make it beautiful by embroidering it with flowers,
As if a pretty girl adorned with the seven treasures were to emerge from behind a screen,

Or the full moon from behind a cloud;
To make [the audience] laugh with his eyes.
Good looks are inborn,
And can't be changed.
These are the requirements for *p'ansori* singers.
(*Kwangdae Song*, adapted from Song B.S.(2) pp.103 - 4)

Mo Hung-gap, the singer depicted in plate 133, was one of the greatest *p'ansori* artists of the 19th century. The *Kwangdae Song* likens him to the famous Chinese poet Du Fu : "[His voice] is like the wind among trees in the moonlit Mount Kwan, or the hooping of a crane in the clear sky."

PLATE 135 Sin Yun-bok, *Sword dance*. Album leaf. 28.3 × 35.2 cms. *Kansong Museum of Fine Arts, Seoul*

The instruments shown in this picture are (left to right) *haegŭm*, [*p'iri*], *taegŭm*, *changgo*, *puk*.

PLATE 136 Sin Yun-bok, *Music and dance*. Album leaf. 28.3 × 35.2 cms. *National Museum, Seoul*

The instruments shown in this picture are (left to right) *changgo*, *p'iri*, *p'iri*, *haegŭm*.

PLATE 137 Sin Yun-bok, *Musical ensemble*. Album leaf. 28.3 × 35.2 cms. *National Museum, Seoul*

The instruments shown in this picture are (left to right) *taegŭm*, *haegŭm*, *kŏmun'go*.

PLATE 138 Attr. An Kyŏn (brush-name Hyŏndongja, 1418 - ?), *Landscape at Chipi* 161.5 × 102.3 cms. *National Museum, Seoul*

PLATE 139 Detail of the above

The figure seated in the centre of the boat holds a set of *so* (panpipes).

PLATE 140 Sin Yun-bok, *Boating scene*. Album leaf. 28.3 × 35.2 cms. *National Museum, Seoul*

The instruments seen in this picture are a *taegŭm* (left) and a *saenghwang* (right).

PLATE 141 Kim Sŏk-sin (1758 - ?), *Music and dance in mid-stream* (detail). 31.6 × 41.9 cms. *Son Seki Collection*

The instruments seen in the rear boat in this picture are (left to right) *puk*, vertical flute, *haegŭm*, *taegŭm*, *p'iri*, *changgo*.

PLATE 142 Further detail of the above

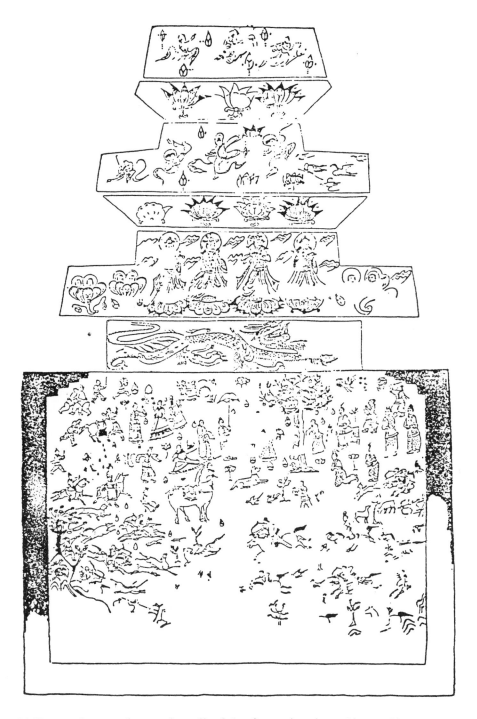

Fig. 51 Decoration on the north wall of the front chamber, Chang Chuan no. 1 tomb

Notes to pp. 191~253

1. For an illustration of the *yo* (Ch. *nao*) in a Han mounted band see Yang *(1)* pl.35. Hayashi Minao *(1)* fig.9 - 7 shows another example but wrongly identifies it as a *chaeng* (Ch. *zheng*).

2. The instrument had made an earlier appearance on a Han mural of a mounted procession at Xiaotangshan. See E.Chavannes, *Mission archéologique dans la Chine septrionale,* Paris 1909, pl.25. It has been referred to as a kind of flute (Mun & Mun *(1)* p.6), but its connection with the horn is correctly affirmed by Yang *(1)* p.128.

3. Wang Chengli, *Pohai jianshi,* Heilongjiang chubanshi, 1982.

4. Diagrams and illustrations for 1828 and 1829, however, show no screens on the terrace, and the musicians appear to have an uninterrupted view of everything in front of them.

5. L.H.Underwood, *Fifteen years among the top-knots,* Boston, 1904, p.94.

6. ed. Yi Son-kun, *T'amna hunyŏkto,* repr. Academy of Korean Studies, Seoul, 1977.

7. Another hint of the King's desire to confirm proper filial relationships is provided by his support for Pak Che-ga, a scholar who returned from China in 1778 and wrote against those who still condemned ties with Manchu China. Pak urged the acquisition of practical knowledge from China for Korea's benefit, and if there was some potential conflict between the pragmatic approach of the *sirhak* school and the obedience demanded by a truly filial relationship, King Chongjo at least seems to have been glad to demonstrate his appreciation of Chinese scholarship and expertise.

8. *SS* 8, p.160.

9. 1607, 1617, 1624, 1636, 1643, 1655, 1682, 1711, 1719, 1748, 1764, 1811. See Kusano Taeko, 'Unknown aspects of Korean influence on Japanese folk music', in Yearbook (1) pp.31-37. For the exchange of diplomatic missions between Korea and Japan see Yi Chin-hui, 'Korean envoys and Japan: Korean-Japanese relations in the 17th to 19th centuries', *KJ* vol.25 no.12, 1985.

10. See for example the mural from cave 320. *Dunhuang di ishu baozang,* Hongkong 1980, p1.73.

11. *Sejong sillok* ch.27 p.26. Details of Pak Yŏn's career in this note are taken from this and succeeding chapters.

12. The history of *p'yŏngsaengdo* has not yet been written, but a connection may be seen with the example of very early tomb art in fig.51, which also shows details of daily human life and entertainment surmounted by an impression of heavenly glories.

13. Chang & Li *(1).*

14. At Namtongri, Sangchukun, Kyŏngsang Pukto. See *Taishō shichinendo koseki chōsa hōkoku,* 1, 1918, pl.28 no.53.

15. *SGSG* 32.6a ff.

16. Jilin Sheng Wenwu Gongzuodui, 'Jian Changchuan yihao bihuamu', *DKYL,* 1982 Pt.1, p.163.

17. Huang Qishan, 'Songdai huaqiang yaogu', *Yueqi* 1983 Pt.3, p.14. See also Hayashi Kenzo *(1)* pp.106 - 123, 'Gezhong xi yaogu'.

18. Korean Central History Museum, *Koguryŏ pyŏkhwa,* P'yŏngyang 1979, pp.66 - 7.

19. *Korea Newsreview,* 21 April 1984 p.23.

20. Two contemporary Chinese bells, also of great size, are preserved in the provincial museums at Xi'an (711 A.D.) and Jinan (751 A.D.). Neither can match those of Sangwŏnsa and Pongdŏksa in the quality of their decoration.

21. One of the earliest representations of a deva playing a two-stringed fiddle is in cave 10 of the Yuan dynasty Yulin Grottoes at Dunhuang. Plate 93 shows a rare example of a Korean deva playing the *haegŭm.*

22. *Han'guk misul ch'ongjip,* Tonghwa Publishing Co., Seoul 1973; vol.12 pls.82, 83.

23. My Love's the mountain range,
    The valleys each with solitary grove,
    The islands far and strange,
    The streams with sounds that change,
    The whistling of the lovesick winds that rove.
    Before the dawn comes round
    Here is the night, dead-hushed with all its glamours,
    The music without sound,

The solitude that clamours,

…(tr. Roy Campbell, *St. John of the Cross*: *Poems*, Penguin Books Ltd., 1960, p.35).

24. B. Watson, *The complete works of Chuang Tzu*, Columbia University Press 1968, pp.157–8.

25. *SGSG* Ch.32.

26. Kim W.Y., *Studies on Silla pottery*, Seoul 1960, pp.98–9.

27. Chŏn C.N *(2)*, pp.91–2.

28. A late Han tomb mural from Dahuting, Mixian, Henan Province shows a long *jue* horn accompanying a dancer (above, fig.30, top). *Wenwu* 1972 no.10 f.p.40.

29. E. Chavannes, *op.cit.*, pl.83 bottom. A fine mural in a Jin dynasty tomb at Jiayuguan, Jiuquan, Gansu Province, shows dancers accompanied by a *guqin, pipa, qiangdi* and *yaogu* (*Wenwu* 1979 no.6, f.p.16).

30. As part of the *sirhak* movement some landscape painters did put emphasis on the precise representation of Korean scenery. Ch'ŏng Son (see plates 48–50) was the most renowned of them.

31. Their predecessors appear on a Japanese painting of the 8th century in the Shōsōin Treasury (Shōsōin *(1)* pls.196–9). Painted at a time when Chinese and Korean cultural influences were strong in Japan, it shows the procession of an itinerant entertainment troupe.

32. See Chae Hui-wan, '*Sinmyŏng* as an artistic experience in traditional Korean group performance plays', *KJ* vol.22 no.5, 1983, pp.4–14.

Bibliography A

Works cited in the text and notes

Cao Z. (1), 'A discussion of the history of the *guzheng*', (tr. Y. Knobloch), *AM* XIV - 2 1982, pp. 1-16

Chang S.H. *(1), Han'guk akki taegwan*, Seoul 1969
    (2), 'Court orchestral music', *SKATM* pp. 181-201
    (3), 'Art song', *SKATM* pp. 181-201

Chang S.H. & Li C.X. *(1), Dunhuang fei tian*, Beijing 1980

Cho H.Y. & Prunner G. *(1), Kisan Pungsok doch'op*, Pumyang Pub. Co., Seoul, 1984

Chŏn C.N. *(1)*, 'Research into the musical instruments in Koguryŏ tomb paintings' (in Korean), *Munhwa yusan* 1, Feb. 1957 P'yŏngyang, pp. 41-71, and 2, April 1957, pp. 26-33 *(2)*, Ditto (in Chinese translation) *Yinyue yanjiu*, 1959 no. 9, pp. 85-104; 1959 no. 10, pp. 87-91

Chu C.G. *(1)*, 'A study of the artistic activities of the people of Koguryŏ' (in Korean), *Kogo minsok nonmunjip* 8, 1983 P'yŏngyang, pp. 237-260

Chuang P.L. *(1), Chung-kuo ku-tai chih fei-hsiao*, Taipei 1963

Condit J. (1), 'The evolution of *Yŏmillak* from the fifteenth century to the present day', *AAM* pp. 231-264
    (2), 'Two Song-dynasty Chinese tunes preserved in Korea', *MT* pp. 1-40
    (3), *Music of the Korean renaissance*, Cambridge University Press 1983
    (4), 'Korean scores in the modified fifteenth century mensural notation', *MA* 4, Cambridge 1984

DeWoskin K.J. (1), *A song for one or two*, Ann Arbor, Michigan 1982

Eckardt A. *(1), Koreanische Musik*, Leipzig 1930

Hahn M.Y. (1), 'Buddhist chant', *SKATM* pp.161-174

Hayashi K. *(1), Dongya yueqi kao,* Beijing 1962

Hayashi M. *(1), Kandai no bunbutsu,* Kyoto 1976

Heyman A. (1), *Dances of the three-thousand league land,* Seoul 1966
    (2), 'Mooka, the shaman song of Korea', *KC* vol.1 no.1, 1984

Huhm H.P. (1), *Korean shaman rituals,* Hollym Intnl. Corp., New York 1980

Kim T.G. (1), 'Shamanistic chants', *SKAFA* pp.115-136

Korean National Commission for UNESCO, *Traditional performing arts of Korea,* Seoul 1975

Lee B.H. (1), *'P'ansori', SKATM* pp.212-228
    (2), 'Shamanistic music', *SKATM* pp.175-180
    (3), *'P'ansori', SKAFA* pp.295-305

Lee D.H. (1), 'Mask-dance drama', *SKAFA* pp.137-165
    (2), 'Korean masks and mask-dance plays', *TKBRAS* 42, 1966 pp.49-67

Lee H.K. *(1), Han'guk ŭmak yŏn'gu,* Seoul 1957
    (2), *A history of Korean music,* Seoul 1970
    (3), (tr.R.Provine) ' Musical paintings in a fourth-century Korean tomb', *KJ* vol.14 no.3, 1974, pp.4-14
    (4), 'Introduction to Korean music', *KJ* vol.16 no.12, 1976, pp.4-14
    (5), Han'guk ŭmak nonch'ong, Seoul 1976
    (6), (translated into modern Korean with commentary) *Akhak kwebŏm,* 2 vols., Seoul 1980
    (7), (tr.R.Provine) *Essays on Korean traditional music,* Seoul 1981

Lee P.H. (1), *Songs of flying dragons: a critical reading,* Harvard University Press 1975

Mun H.Y. & Mun C.S. *(1), Chaoxian yinyue,* Beijing 1962

National Academy of Arts (1), *Survey of traditional Korean arts: traditional music,* Seoul 1973
    (2), *Survey of traditional Korean arts: folk arts,* Seoul 1974

Pratt K.L. (1), 'Music as a factor in Sung-Koryŏ diplomatic relations, 1069-1126', *T'oung Pao* LXII 4-5 1976, pp.199-217

Provine R.C. (1), 'Sejong and the preservation of Chinese ritual melodies', *KJ* vol.14 no.2, 1974, pp.34-39

BIBLIOGRAPHY A

    (2), 'The sacrifice to Confucius in Korea and its music', *TKBRAS* 50, 1975, pp.43-69

    (3), (tr.F.P.Nellen) 'Die rhythmischen Strukturen in der Koreanischen Folklore', *Korea Kulturmagazin,* Bonn 1982 no.1, pp.33-50

Shōsōin *(1)*, *Shōsōin no gakki,* Tokyo 1967

Song B.S. *(1)*, *Akchang tŭngnok yŏn'gu,* Yŏngnam University 1980

    (2), *Source readings in Korean music,* Korean National Commission for UNESCO 1980

Song K.R. (1), 'The Confucius *(sic)* temple music', *SKATM* pp.142-150

    (2), 'The royal ancestral shrine music', *SKATM* pp.150-160

Sur D. (1), 'A conspectus of modes in Korean music', *KC* vol.1 no.1, 1980, pp.14-16

Widdess D.R. & Wolpert R.F. eds. (1), *Music and tradition: essays on Asian and other musics,* Cambridge University Press 1981

Williamson M.C. (1), 'The iconography of arched harps in Burma', *MT* pp.209-228

Wu Z. & Liu D.S. *(1)*, *Zhongguo yinyue shilue,* Beijing 1983

Yang Y.L. *(1)*, *Zhongguo gudai yinyue shikao,* Beijing 1980

Yearbook (1), *Yearbook for traditional music,* vol.15, 1983 (Korean music issue), International Council for Traditional Music, New York

Zhongguo *(1)*, *Zhongguo yinyue shi cankao tupian,* vol.9, 'Beichao di jiyuetian he jiyueren', Beijing 1964

Bibliography B

Works on Korean and related musics not cited in the text

Articles on Asian music: *Festschrift for Dr Chang Sa-hun,* Korean Musicological Society, Seoul 1977

Asian Music IX-2 (Korean music issue), Society for Asian Music, New York, 1978

Chang S.H., *Kugak non'go,* Seoul 1971
    , *Han'guk chŏnt'ong ŭmak ŭi yŏn'gu,* Seoul 1975
    , *Kugak ch'ongnon,* Seoul 1976
    , *Han'guk ŭmaksa,* Seoul 1976
    , *Han'guk chŏnt'ong muyong yŏn'gu,* Seoul 1977
    , *Sejongjo ŭmak yŏn'gu,* Seoul 1982
    , *Kugak taesajŏn,* Seoul 1984

Condit J., 'A fifteenth century Korean score in mensural notation', *MA* 2, 1979, pp.1-87

Kim H.K. ed., *Studies on Korea, a scholar's guide,* Hawaii 1980; 'music' pp.187-191, 'drama and dance' pp.192-3

Kishibe S., *Tōdai ongaku shi no kenkyū,* Tokyo 1960-61
    , *Tenpyō no hibiki 729-749,* Tokyo 1984

Kishibe S. & Hayashi K., *Tōdai no gakki,* Tokyo 1968

Lee B.W., 'A short history of *pŏmp'ae*', *Journal of Korean Studies* vol.1 (2), 1971, pp.109-121
    , 'Structural formulae of melodies in the two sacred Buddhist styles of Korea', *Korean Studies,* 1, 1977, pp.111- 196
    , 'Micro- and macro-structure of melody and rhythm in Korean Buddhist chant', *KJ* vol.22 no.3, 1982, pp.33-38

BIBLIOGRAPHY B

Lee H.K., 'Quintuple meter in Korean instrumental music', *AM* XIII-l, 1982, pp.119-129

Malm W.P., *Music cultures of the Pacific, the Near East and Asia,* Prentice Hall Inc., 2nd ed., 1977

Mitani Y., *Tō Ajia kinso no kenkyū,* Tokyo 1978

Nellen F.P., *Bibliographie zu Musik und Tanz im traditionellen Korea, Teil A, Literatur in Europais-chen Sprachen,* Bochum 1984

New Grove dictionary of music and musicians, MacMillan & Co, 1982, article on 'Korea'

Pak P.S., *Chosŏn-jo ŭi ŭigwe,* Seoul 1985

Picken, L. *et al., Music from the Tang court,* vol.l Oxford University Press 1981, vols.2-3 Cambridge University Press 1985

Pratt K.L., 'Sung Hui Tsung's musical diplomacy and the Korean response', *Bulletin of the School of Oriental and African Studies,* XLIV/3, 1981, pp.509-521

Provine R.C., *Drum rhythms in Korean farmers' music,* Seoul 1975
, '"Chinese" ritual music in Korea : the origins, codification, and cultural role of aak', *KJ* vol.20 no.2, 1980, pp.16-25

Rockwell C., *Kagok, a traditional Korean vocal form,* Providence, Rhode Island 1972
, 'Kayago: the origin and evolution of the Korean twelve-string zither', *TKBRAS* 49, 1974 pp.26-47

Song B.S., *Korean music: an annotated bibliography,* Providence, Rhode Island 1971; supplements in *KJ* vol.14 no.12-vol.15 no.4 and *AM* IX-2 1978
, 'The etymology of the Korean six-stringed zither, kŏmun'go, a critical review', *KJ* vol.15 no.10, 1975, pp.18-23
, 'A discography of Korean music', *AM* VIII-2, 1977, pp.82-121
, *Han'guk ŭmakhak nonjŏ haeje,* Sŏngnamsi, Kyŏnggido 1981
, *Han'guk ŭmak t'ongsa,* Seoul 1984
, *Han'guk kodae ŭmaksa yŏn'gu,* Seoul 1985

Song K.R., 'Korean court dance', *KJ* vol.16 no.12, 1976, pp.20-28

Tanabe H., *Chūgoku Chōsen ongaku chōsa kikō,* Tokyo 1970

Walraven B.C.A., *Muga, the songs of Korean shamanism,* Leiden 1985

Bibliography C

Korean art

Choi S.U., *Five thousand years of Korean art,* Seoul 1979

Goepper R. & Whitfield R., *Treasures from Korea,* British Museum, London 1984

Han'guk misul ch'ongjip, 15 vols., Tonghwa Pub. Co., Seoul 1973

Han'guk ŭi mi, 24 vols., Chungang Ilbosa, Seoul 1985

Kim C.W. & Kim W.Y., *The arts of Korea,* Thames & Hudson 1966

Kim C.W. & Lee L.K., *Arts of Korea,* Kodansha International 1974

Kim H.K., ed., *Studies on Korea: a scholar's guide,* Hawaii 1980; 'art' pp.176-186

Ministry of Culture & Information, *The arts of ancient Korea,* Seoul 1974

The National Treasures of Korea, 12 vols., Yekyong Pub. Co., Seoul 1985

Glossary - Index of Musical and Artistic Names and Terms

(A) KOREAN

aak 雅樂 아악 17, 32, 35, 37, 40, 44, 47, 55, 66, 68, 69, 202, 208, 215, 216, 231
ajaeng 牙箏 아쟁 46, 47, 63, 66, 71, 72, 74, 204
Akhak kwebŏm 樂學軌範 악학궤범 40, 64, 66, 69, 77, 78, 85, 91, 202, 207, 208, 216, 231, 233, 243, 247, 249
An Kyŏn 安堅 안견 *188,* 248, 252

chaeng 鉦 쟁 255
chajinmori 자진모리 56, 57, 58, *59*
changdan 長短 장단 57, 58, *59*
changgo 杖鼓 장고 46, 47, 49, 52, 54, 57, 85, 86 - 7, 204, 206, 208, 210, 211, 213, 227, 229, 233, 249, 252, 253
changjŏk 長笛 장적 219, 242, 248
chapka 雜歌 잡가 41, 52
chapsaek 雜色 잡색 53
chego 齋鼓 재고 88
chi 箎 지 28, 80, 88
Chin Che - hai 秦再奚 진재해 *180,* 249
Chinch'an ŭigwe 進饌儀軌 진찬의궤 203
Chinjak ŭigwe 進爵儀軌 진작의궤 203
ching 鉦 징 47, 52, 204, 206
chin'go 晋鼓 진고 67, 84
chingyangjo 진양조 41, 51, 56, 57, 58, *59*
chissori 짓소리 50, 51
chŏ (horizontal flute) 邃 저 *141, 144, 150,* 197, 211, 219, 220, 227
chŏk 笛 적 88, 249
chŏngak 正樂 정악 46, 47, 49
Chŏngdaeŏp 中大葉 중대엽 35, 38
chŏngganbo 井間譜 정간보 *60 - 61,* 62
Chŏngmyoak 宗廟樂 종묘악 193
chunggŭm 中苓 중금 29

264

(B) CHINESE

Korean   Temple   Names

Chogyesa 曹溪寺 조계사
Ch'injŏnsa 陳田寺 진전사
Hwaŏmsa 華嚴寺 화엄사
Kamŭnsa 感恩寺 감은사
Kapsa 甲寺 갑사
Pang'wŏnsa 奉元寺 봉원사
Pŏmŏsa 梵魚寺 범어사
Pongamsa 鳳岩寺 봉암사
Pongdŏksa 奉德寺 봉덕사
Pŏpchusa 法住寺 법주사
Pulguksa 保國寺 보국사
Sangwŏnsa 上院寺 상원사
Songgwangsa 松廣寺 송광사
Sŏngnamsa 石南寺 석남사
T'ongdosa 通度寺 통도사
Yongamsa 龍岩寺 용암사
Yŏngjusa 龍珠寺 용주사

Picture Credits and Acknowledgments

Ahn C.H., Cat.nos. 1,3-5 (top), 6-11, 20-22; pls.4, 6-7, 10, 12-18, 24-25, 29-30, 38, 41-43, 45-46, 51-52, 57-59, 61-62, 64-66, 77, 80-85, 88, 92, 97-98, 101, 105-106, 119, 122, 124, 127, 130

Asian Art Museum of San Francisco, the Avery Brundage Collection, pl.126

British Museum, by courtesy of the Trustees, Fig.46

Dr. Cho Hung-youn, pl. 11

Ewha Women's University Museum, pl.107

Kim T.B., Cat.nos. 2, 12-14; pls. 3, 8-9, 35, 74-75, 123, 125, 129, 135

National Classical Music Institute, Seoul, Cat.5 (bottom); pl.5

National Museum, Seoul, pls.26-28, 54, 102-103, 114, 118, 138-139

K.P., Cat.nos. 18-19; pls. 1-2, 31-34, 37, 39-40, 44, 47-50, 55-56, 60, 63, 67-69, 72, 76, 89-91, 93-94, 96, 99, 104, 120, 131, 133, 141-142

Rachel Pratt, Fig.28

Jean Provine, Cat.17

Shōsōin Treasure-house, by Courtesy of the Office of the, pl.19

Professor Song Bang-song, pl.79

Sungjon University Museum, pls.113, 134

For permission to quote words and music from *Music of the Korean renaissance,* the author and publishers wish to express their thanks to the Syndics of the Cambridge University Press.

General Index

278